THE BOGGART AND THE MONSTER

ALSO BY SUSAN COOPER

The Boggart

The Boggart Fights Back

The Dark Is Rising Sequence

Over Sea, Under Stone

The Dark Is Rising

Greenwitch

The Grey King

Silver on the Tree

Ghost Hawk

King of Shadows

Green Boy

Seaward

Victory

The Magician's Boy

The Silver Cow

A BOGGART BOOK

THE BOGGART AND THE MONSTER

SUSAN COOPER

Margaret K. McElderry Books

New York London Toronto Sydney New Delhi

MARGARET K. McELDERRY BOOKS

An imprint of Simon & Schuster Children's Publishing Division

1230 Avenue of the Americas, New York, New York 10020

This book is a work of fiction. Any references to historical events, real people, or real places are used fictitiously. Other names, characters, places, and events are products of the author's imagination, and any resemblance to actual events or places or persons, living or dead, is entirely coincidental.

Text copyright © 1997 by Susan Cooper

Cover illustration copyright © 2018 by Stacy Curtis

All rights reserved, including the right of reproduction in whole or in part in any form.

MARGARET K. McELDERRY BOOKS is a trademark of Simon & Schuster, Inc.

For information about special discounts for bulk purchases, please contact Simon & Schuster Special Sales at 1-866-506-1949 or business@simonandschuster.com.

The Simon & Schuster Speakers Bureau can bring authors to your live event. For more information or to book an event, contact the Simon & Schuster Speakers Bureau at 1-866-248-3049 or visit our website at www.simonspeakers.com.

The text for this book was set in Berkeley Medium.

Manufactured in the United States of America

0118 OFF

This Margaret K. McElderry Books paperback edition February 2018

2 4 6 8 10 9 7 5 3 1

The Library of Congress has cataloged the hardcover edition as follows:

Cooper, Susan.

The boggart and the monster / Susan Cooper—1st ed.

p.   cm.

Summary: In this companion volume to *The Boggart*, the invisible and mischievous spirit living in the Scottish Castle Keep sets out to help save Nessie the Loch Ness Monster, one of his few remaining cousins.

ISBN 978-0-689-81330-6 (hardcover)

ISBN 978-0-689-84784-4 (eBook)

[1. Supernatural—Fiction. 2. Loch Ness Monster—Fiction. 3. Scotland—Fiction.] I. Title.

PZ7.C7878Br 1997   [Fic]—dc22   96-42389

ISBN 978-1-5344-2012-0 (pbk)

For Zoë
dear friend

AUTHOR'S NOTE

The geography of this book is very nearly truthful, but not quite; I have taken a few liberties with the shape of Port Appin's coastline, and the land surrounding Loch Ness. And as in a book called *The Boggart*, I ask forgiveness from the owners of Castle Stalker and of the Appin Community Cooperative Store for turning their homes into Castle Keep and the Camerons' village shop.

The Boggart is not related to Humphrey Bogart; the "o" in his name is short, as in "dog." The name Urquhart, for anyone who has never come across it, is pronounced Erkut.

I am very grateful once more to Charles Dunn for the Boggart's Gaelic, and to my son Jonathan for his patient and invaluable advice on underwater research.

into his mug, poured on the hot milk, and stirred, sniffing gratefully at the comforting sweet smell. Then he looked up—and made a small horrified noise like a strangled hiccup.

A few inches from his nose, another spoon, also mounded with Ovaltine powder, was rising alone through the air, rapidly but steadily. As he watched, it hovered for a moment and the Ovaltine in it suddenly vanished—and the spoon, empty again, fell with a clatter to the floor.

Mr. Maconochie slowly put down his mug on the kitchen table, and bent and picked up the fallen spoon. It was perfectly clean. He groaned softly, and shook his head. More and more often in the months since he had moved into Castle Keep, he had been seeing things happen that were impossible. Small, insignificant, meaningless things; things so small that it was possible each time for him to wonder if he hadn't imagined what he saw. Mr. Maconochie had been a lawyer before he retired and bought Castle Keep, and forty years in the Edinburgh courts had made him a rational, cool-headed man. If he was sure of nothing else, he was sure that everything that happens in this world has a reason: that stolen property vanishes because somebody has taken it; that a murdered man dies because somebody has killed him. When with no reason at all he saw a spoon rise vertically into the air, and a spoonful of brown powder suddenly disappear, he knew at once that one of two fates had befallen him: either something terrible was happening to his eyesight, or he was going mad.

His golden Labrador dog, William, stirred, where he had been sleeping in the warm kitchen corner beside the stove, and stretched. Then he loped over to Mr. Maconochie and licked his hand, waving his tail. He was a cheerful, affectionate dog, three years old but a puppy at heart. Mr. Maconochie rubbed his head, grateful for company. Then suddenly he let out a shout, and William a shrill resentful yelp—for William's feathery golden tail had shot vertically up in the air, straight as a ruler, in a movement quite impossible for a dog to achieve on his own.

The tail stood stiffly upright for a few seconds, while William turned in a circle, whining in protest. Then just as suddenly, it dropped again. William stopped turning and waved it a little, experimentally, looking reproachfully at Mr. Maconochie.

Mr. Maconochie stared wildly up at the ceiling, hoping for a desperate moment that he might see a string cunningly rigged up by his two small great-nephews, as a delayed-action device to grab unsuspecting dogs' tails. But there was nothing to be seen, and anyway the nephews hadn't been near the castle since their Easter vacation, three months before. There was no help for it: he had to accept the fact that *somebody invisible had pulled his dog's tail.*

"Oh dear me," said Mr. Maconochie. He reached for his Ovaltine and took an unhappy swig.

William licked his hand forgivingly.

With the dog trotting beside him, Mr. Maconochie went out of the kitchen along the bright corridor to the library. In all its long history the castle had been a place of dark corners and dim lamplit rooms, but now electric lights blazed welcomingly from the forbidding stone walls. Mr. Maconochie liked light, just as he liked rational explanations, so he had replaced the flames of all the ancestral candlesticks and paraffin lamps with a little Japanese diesel generator, which chugged away merrily and almost inaudibly in the castle's dungeon, powering electric lights, toaster and Mr. Maconochie's aging electric typewriter.

Seeking both light and reason now, Mr. Maconochie went into the library, a wonderfully lofty room lined with tall bookcases and furnished with the heavy desk and big leather armchairs that the MacDevon had loved. Devon MacDevon had been the last owner of Castle Keep, and the last chieftain of the MacDevon clan; he had fallen peacefully asleep for the last time in the castle three years earlier, at the age of 102. All his books were still here in this book-lined retreat, and Mr. Maconochie had spent blissful hours dipping into them, marveling at the range of the MacDevon's interests. Not only were there quantities of historical tomes about the MacDevon clan, books for which he had recently been offered large sums of money by a Scottish-named college in Texas; there were thousands of others, in immense variety. Mr. Maconochie often wished he could have met the old man before he died; he knew he would have enjoyed the acquaintance of someone whose curiosity spanned subjects as varied as the migration patterns of the lesser crested grebe, the late clarinet quintets of Brahms, fourteenth-century Scottish crofting and the history of ice cream.

Swallowing another gulp of Ovaltine, he set his mug down on the MacDevon's big mahogany desk and took a large flashlight from the drawer. Even the new electric lights, he knew, were not strong enough to reach the furthest corners and the highest shelves of the library. Then, armed with the flashlight, he began roaming along shelf after shelf of books, peering at titles, until he came at last to the group he was looking for. Tucked away on a high shelf, they all dealt with ghosts and the supernatural. Mr. Maconochie balanced precariously on the top rung of the wooden library stepladder and pulled out a leather-bound volume entitled *Hauntings of the Scottish Highlands and Islands.*

He climbed down the ladder and stood there for a moment, contemplating the cover of the book. *You're a sensible fellow, James,* said a small disapproving voice in his head. *You're a lawyer, man. What the devil are you doing reading a rubbishy book like this?* For a moment, he almost climbed back up the ladder and put the book back where it belonged. But the image of the hovering spoonful of Ovaltine flickered back into his mind, and he knew it was not going to go away—and that the small disapproving voice had nothing to say that would help. Shaking his head despondently, he crossed the room and settled himself at the big desk. William lay curled up in front of the fireplace, twitching in his sleep. The wind outside had dropped, and the room was very still, with no sound but the soft lapping of the waves, far below the window, against the rocks of the islet on which the castle stood.

Mr. Maconochie turned the thick crackling pages. The book was set out alphabetically, and he leafed through sections on the ghost of Aberdeen Castle, the great white Auk of the Firth of Forth, the bloody Axe that appeared each year on the anniversary of the beheading of King Charles I, and the wailing Baby heard every Hogmanay near Hadrian's Wall. Then he came to a section headed *Boggarts*.

He read, "Kin to a brownie, a boggart is a house spirit of no malice but of endless mischief. Found exclusively in Scotland and the North of England, he is above all—"

Mr. Maconochie turned the page, to read the rest. But lying on the next page, tucked into the binding of the book, he found an envelope. It was sealed, and on the flap was the crest of the MacDevon family. When he turned it over, he found it was addressed, in a flowing, delicate, scholarly hand:

"To the New Owner of Castle Keep."

Mr. Maconochie stared at the envelope, overwhelmed by an emotion like nothing he had ever felt before. It was as though an unknown voice were calling his name, out of the past or perhaps the future. He found that his glasses were suddenly misty, so he took them off and polished them with his handkerchief. On the hearthrug, William stirred and whimpered in his sleep. Mr. Maconochie reached for the MacDevon's letter-opener, a long slim dagger carved from the antler of a deer, and carefully slit the envelope open.

There was only one sheet inside, written on crested paper in the same graceful old-fashioned hand. It had no date or greeting; it simply began:

"So you've found him. And you have an intelligent head on your shoulders if you've come to this room and this book to find what to do. I'd have liked to meet you.

"Don't be feared of him. He means no harm, but his tricks will drive you wild if you let them. Be patient. He's older than you or me or the castle or the clan, and he'll be here when we're all gone. He's a thieving rascal, but he eats seldom and little. He likes porridge and cream and new wholemeal bread, apples and cheese, ice cream, ketchup, pickled onions, and fish. Fish above all—he is kin to the seals, as are we MacDevons. And like us too, he enjoys his dram. But if you're short of whisky, he has a great taste for Ovaltine."

Mr. Maconochie looked at his mug, which he had left half-full on the desk before him. It was empty. He stared wildly around the room, but saw no sign of life anywhere, no flicker of light or sound.

He looked back at the page, at the letter from dead Devon MacDevon, and read on.

"He's a good soul, but he'll forget me when I'm gone. There's not but a few left like him, cousins here and there, not many. Have him stay, if you can. He's the Boggart of Castle Keep, and I'm fond of him.

"Good luck to you."

Then there was a line in Gaelic, which Mr. Maconochie, though Scottish born and bred, could not translate, and a flowing signature, "MacDevon." And that was all.

Mr. Maconochie looked out across the library, at the books and the fading family portraits, and the stone walls that had been standing for five hundred years and more. He said in a husky tentative voice, "Boggart? Are you there?"

From a high shelf in the far wall, in shadow from the light, he heard a thread of a laugh.

* * *

MOVING DOWN THE DARKENED aisle with her tray, the flight attendant noticed that Jessup was wide awake. She smiled at him. "Water?" she whispered. "Coke?"

"Water," said Jessup. "Thanks."

He reached past his sleeping sister Emily for the little plastic glass, and knocked it back in one gulp. The flight attendant grinned, exchanged it wordlessly for a full one, and moved on.

Jessup stretched, sighed, drank his second glass of water, and switched off the little television screen in front of his seat. It had shown him one long unfunny comic film made ten years ago, when he was two, and now it was starting another, and Jessup had had enough. He seemed to be the only wakeful person in this part of the plane. Across the aisle his parents were propped against each other, deep in sleep; on his left Emily had been curled up in an unconscious ball ever since dinner, and the man on his right was snoring softly, like an elderly dog.

Jessup looked at his watch. Two hours to London. He peered at the window beyond his neighbor, but saw only transatlantic darkness and the steady flash of the light on the airplane's wing. Then his eyes dropped to the open book lying facedown on the sleeping man's lap. *Hunting the Loch Ness Monster,* said the title in aggressive dark print. Beneath it was a picture of a monstrous creature half-submerged in a lake, with a huge body from which rose a long, curving neck, and a wide-open mouth filled with terrifyingly sharp teeth.

Jessup brightened. Next-best to computers, he loved stories about monsters. He reached out a stealthy hand and removed the book.

Forty minutes later he was deep in reading when another flight attendant came by, this time with a tray of glasses of orange juice. She was less cautious than the last. "Juice, anyone?" she enquired, brightly and loudly.

Emily didn't stir, but the man in the window seat said thickly, "Uuurrgh," and held out his hand without opening his eyes. Jessup watched in fascination as he took and drank the orange juice while apparently still asleep. He was a chunky, middle-aged man with a shining bald head fringed by stringy grey hair, and wire-rimmed glasses hanging from a string around his neck. He was wearing faded jeans, sneakers and a rather grubby college basketball sweatshirt. Suddenly he opened his eyes and caught Jessup studying him, and he grinned. It was an engaging, friendly grin, showing a piratical gold tooth at one side of his mouth.

"Greetings," he said.

"Hi," said Jessup. He looked down guiltily at his lap. "Uh—I borrowed your book."

"Feel free," said the man equably. "Did you enjoy it?"

"It's great!" said Jessup, with honest fervor.

The man grinned again. "That's an excellent answer," he said. "I wrote it."

"You wrote this?" Jessup looked down at the front cover. "You're Harold Pindle Sc.D.?"

"Call me Harold," said the man. He held out a large callused hand, and Jessup's considerably smaller fist was swallowed up in a firm handshake. "I'm Jessup Volnik," Jessup said.

"Well met in midair, Jessup Volnik," said Harold.

"You really think the Loch Ness Monster is a plesiosaur?" said Jessup.

Harold looked at him for a long moment, and then sighed wistfully. "You know, Jessup," he said, "I have four daughters, and not one of them would be capable of asking a beautiful question like that at first meeting. Clearly the thing that is missing in my life is a son—a son just like you."

Jessup eyed him warily. "A *beautiful* question?" he said.

"The lovely natural assumption that the Monster is a fact," said Harold. "The first thing most people say, including my rational daughters, is, 'You really *believe* in the Loch Ness Monster?'"

"I'm good at believing in things," Jessup said. "But—a plesiosaur—"

"I'm convinced of it," said Harold warmly. "It's the only theory that fits with the sightings, so far as you can trust them. Aquatic creature, air-breathing, cold-blooded, fish-eating, huge body, long neck, small head—did you know the word plesiosaur means 'next to a lizard'?"

Jessup said, "But plesiosaurs have been extinct for sixty thousand years."

"Seventy," said Harold amiably. "And that's what they said about the coelacanth, until some Filipino fisherman caught one in the South Pacific in nineteen fifty-four. I tell you, Jessup, there is absolutely a ple-siosaur in that loch, not just one but a family of them, and I'm going to prove it. I'm heading a new expedi-tion—we start next week. Take a look at this."

He pulled a briefcase from under the seat in front of him, and took out an envelope stuffed with techni-cal leaflets. The envelope, Jessup noticed, was addressed to Professor Harold Pindle, Department of Biology, University of British Columbia. Harold perched his glasses on his nose and spread the leaflets on his tray table. "How about this baby, eh?" he said.

Jessup looked. The leaflets, which appeared to be written in algebra, described a kind of tethered sub-mersible called an ROV, a Remotely Operated Vehicle, like a miniature submarine manned by a computer instead of a person. As if he were talking to a fellow pro-fessor, Harold began happily expounding the merits of ROVs and their parent land-based computers, and Jessup listened. If he had been a normal twelve-year-old, he would have been lost and bored in forty-five seconds flat.

But in one critical respect, Jessup was not a normal twelve-year-old. Though his father was a theater direc-tor and his mother an **antique** dealer, he had been born with a phenomenal gift for computer science, and at weekends he was already taking what were popularly known as "kid genius" classes at the University of Toronto. He began asking Harold a steady stream of increasingly abstruse questions about his computerized submersibles, and Harold happily chattered on, totally disregarding the fact that he appeared to be talking to a child.

An hour later, Emily woke up to find a breakfast tray in front of her, and her young brother deep in conversation with a completely strange man who was talking as though they were contemplating partnership in some technological business enterprise.

"So the strobes can illuminate for twenty-five feet in all directions," Jessup was saying.

"Right," said the man. "And the sonar covers a five-hundred-foot swath."

Emily had been considering her breakfast tray. "Jessup, you want my yogurt?" she said.

Jessup took the offered carton of airline yogurt without pausing for breath. "Awesome—so if the sonar picks up a defined image you can send the ROV in that direction with the strobes. Want Emily's yogurt, Harold?"

"Thank you, Emily," said Harold with his mouth full. He swallowed, and flashed her his cheery gold-toothed grin. Emily eyed his wild fringe of hair and ancient sweatshirt, and smiled back tolerantly. What with Jessup's computer friends and the actors at her father's theater, her life was full of Harolds. She said,

"Are you from the University of Toronto, by any chance?"

"Vancouver," Harold said. "UBC. Harold Pindle, at your service."

"He's going to Scotland to find the Loch Ness Monster," Jessup said. "It's a new expedition with the most amazing instruments. Robot submersibles like the one Robert whatsit used to find the Titanic. I'd give anything to watch."

"Then come visit," Harold said promptly, attacking Emily's carton of yogurt. The rest of his breakfast had vanished, eaten with the speed and abandon of a ravenous seven-year-old. "Are you two on holiday? Where are you staying?"

"Edinburgh, and then Castle Keep," said Jessup with pride.

Emily said, "That's in Argyllshire. Port Appin."

"I should say it is," said Harold warmly. "A major landmark. Beautiful little place."

Jessup paused, and for the first time looked at him with something like disapproval. *"Little?"* he said ominously.

"Well, for a castle," said Harold.

Jessup said stiffly, "We used to *own* Castle Keep. Our father inherited it. From his great-uncle, the last chief of the MacDevon clan." He indicated Robert Volnik, across the aisle, and automatically they all three turned to look at him. Robert was taking a large bite of a bagel, dropping cream cheese into his beard in the process, and looked remarkably unlike a castle-inheritor.

"Ah," said Harold.

"But he sold it to his Scottish lawyer," Emily said. "Mr. Maconochie. So now Mom and Dad are going to the Edinburgh Festival to spend some of their loot, and Jess and I are going to stay with Mr. Mac at the castle. To see . . . old friends."

Harold missed the momentary hesitation in her voice; he was too busy scraping the yogurt carton. "Well, if you feel like taking a day off, Jessup, I'd love to show you the ROVs."

"Tell me some more about the laser line scan." Jessup was off again. Emily sighed, and stopped listening.

She spread cream cheese on her bagel and sat peacefully chewing, watching the sky lighten beyond the airplane's hazy oval windows, thinking of the square granite chunk of Castle Keep, set on its little island in the grey waters of Loch Linnhe. She thought of the nodding pink blossoms of sea-thrift, on the rocks where Tommy Cameron had showed her the seals playing, two years before; she wondered whether Tommy would recognize her now that her hair was cut short, and whether he would find Jessup weird now that his passion for computers had grown even more extreme.

And most of all, she wondered whether the Boggart would remember them.

TWO

✳

"You're an angel to have driven all this way," said Maggie Volnik to Mr. Maconochie outside the King's Head Hotel. His lanky frame was bent over the trunk of his Range Rover, helping Jessup and Robert stow two duffel bags next to a small grandfather clock.

"You certainly are," said Robert. "If I find a play at the Festival that I can produce in Toronto, I shall dedicate it to you."

"Not at all," said Mr. Maconochie. "Every time I come to Edinburgh I pick up some more of my belongings from storage. You'd be amazed how long it takes to move into a castle."

Emily peered at the back seat of his car, half of which was occupied by a large teapot nestling in a blanket. "Think how much more china you could be carrying if you didn't have Jess and me."

"I can't have conversations with china," Mr. Maconochie said. "And I can do things with you and Jessup that I'd never do otherwise, unless my great-nephews were visiting. Swimming, camping, boating—

lovely. Toss a coin, you two, to see who gets the front seat first."

"Take Emily," said Robert. "Jessup falls instantly asleep for the first two hours of any car journey." He and Maggie hugged their children, and shook Mr. Maconochie's hand warmly. It was an amiable parting, with both children and parents contentedly anticipating things the others would neither have enjoyed nor understood. As for Mr. Maconochie, he was simply glad of company.

He repeated this to Emily, as they bowled along the highway, with Jessup, sure enough, fast asleep next to the blanket-swathed teapot.

"Oh *yes*," said Emily sympathetically. "It must be very lonely to be the only person in Castle Keep."

For a wild moment Mr. Maconochie contemplated telling her about the Boggart, but then he lost courage. He knew he had no hope of persuading any intelligent, rational human being that he was being haunted by an invisible house spirit. "I shall be so glad to have you both back in the castle," he said instead.

Emily said casually, "Is Tommy Cameron still around?"

"Oh indeed—I couldn't do without him," Mr. Maconochie said. "He brings all my supplies from his mother's shop, he looks after my boat, he takes William for walks—"

"William?"

"My dog. He's a Labrador. Not too much brain but a lot of energy."

Emily thought: *I bet the Boggart loves playing tricks*

on him— and for a moment she contemplated saying so. But in the next moment she thought better of it. How could she suggest to an intelligent, rational human being that he and his dog were living in a place haunted by an invisible house spirit?

She said, "We're so lucky to *be* back."

And in this state of mutual truth-avoidance they chatted lightly on, as the Highlands unrolled before the window of the traveling car.

* * *

THE SUN WAS DROPPING in the sky when they reached the jetty and parking area of the Camerons' village store in Port Appin. Castle Keep loomed square and black out over the rippling waters of Loch Linnhe, but there was a glint of yellow light here and there in its bulk. The Camerons' store and house, however, were tight-closed and deserted, and there was no sign of Tommy, his parents or their car.

Emily's spirits drooped a little, but not for long. Once she and Jessup were swaying on the water in Mr. Maconochie's little outboard dinghy, she felt she was at home.

The first and only time the Volnik family had come to Castle Keep, it was not an inviting place. Nobody had set foot in it for months after the death of Devon MacDevon, and it was thick with dust and cobwebs and mouse droppings; parts of it were even falling down. Emily and Jessup, previously ecstatic that their father had inherited a real live castle, were disappointed at its unromantic tumbledown state, and their parents were so alarmed that they rapidly began wondering how best to get rid of it.

But in the days that they stayed there, camping out in the kitchen for meals, spending the nights curled in sleeping bags on four-poster beds, Emily and Jessup had fallen in love with Castle Keep. With Tommy Cameron as guide they learned the little bays and beaches of the loch, and the swift-changing moods of its weather, and they looked into the great dark lash-fringed eyes of the seals who came sometimes to the weed-pillowed rocks near the castle.

And the Boggart, glad of new victims, had happily played his tricks on them, though they hadn't noticed him then. Not then, not yet.

Now, coming back to Castle Keep, Emily and Jessup looked around in wonder. The rooms and corridors were not only bright with their new electric lights, they were comfortable. Rugs were spread on the cold stone floors, fires burned in the hearths of several rooms; the kitchen was cozy and welcoming, and warm air from its huge hospitable new stove was piped up to the floor above.

Mr. Maconochie led them proudly up the stairs. "Tommy helped me get things ready," he said. "I do hope you'll be comfortable. You each have your own room this time." And there on the massive oak door of a bedroom was an immaculately lettered sign, in very creditable Times Roman capitals:

JESSUP'S ROOM

Jessup whooped, flung open the door, and dived in, and Mr. Maconochie followed. Emily, shouldering the straps of her duffel, went on to the next door. The sign here said, in a flowing cursive script that looked very like the handwriting of the few letters she had had from Tommy Cameron in the past year:

Emily's Room

Emily opened the door to find a small cheery space, lamps glowing, with bed, desk, armchair, wardrobe, and a thick-walled little window looking out at one bright star in the darkening sky. On a little table beside the bed was a vase holding six red roses, with a card propped underneath: *Welcome back to Scotland.* It was Tommy's handwriting again.

Emily looked at the roses, feeling a strange unfamiliar hollowness in her chest. She swallowed. Nobody had ever given her flowers before.

"Em! Where are you?" She heard Jessup's yell from next door and went hastily out, dropping her duffel bag on the floor.

And the Boggart, delighted at finding a hitherto empty room occupied, dived in through the door as she came out of it. He flittered inquisitively about for a moment, then settled on the duffel, and his long deft invisible fingers began to unfasten the straps.

*　*　*

FROM DOWNSTAIRS, the castle was filled suddenly with

a great eruption of barking, and a flurry of golden limbs and fur came hurtling up the stairs and flung itself on Mr. Maconochie. He protested, staggering. "William—get *down*, William—look, here's Emily and Jessup—"

William leaped happily and indiscriminately at Emily and Jessup, and pranced about in a hysteria of greeting, licking their faces and treading on their toes. Emily staggered down the last few steps, wiping dog-lick out of her eyes, and found herself looking into the amused face of Tommy Cameron.

"Oh—hi, Tommy—" She glanced down, embarrassed, registering in a quick blur that he was much taller than before, his dark hair longer. Jessup and Tommy thumped each other on the shoulder, a procedure for which Jessup had to reach upward and Tommy down. William bounced around them all, delirious with good-fellowship, and Tommy grabbed at his collar.

Then all the lights went out.

In the dark hallway, everyone lapsed into startled silence. Even William's bark dwindled away into a puzzled whine.

"Damn that generator!" said Mr. Maconochie into the darkness.

"But the generator is working fine," Tommy said. "I checked it just this morning when I came to get William." His lilting Highland voice, Emily noticed with fascination, now had a strange husky quality, on its way down the scale to adult depth.

The lights flickered rapidly on and off again, several times.

"That's what it does every day!" said Mr. Maconochie in exasperation. "Every single day, that maddening flicker. I'll have to get the man down from Inverness again."

"Last time he came he said there was nothing wrong," Tommy said.

"And the time before," Mr. Maconochie said. He sighed. "Just a minute—I'll get a torch in case it happens again." He disappeared toward the kitchen.

Emily whispered to Tommy, "It's the Boggart doing that, isn't it? How come Mr. Mac hasn't found out about him yet?"

"He doesn't want to know," Tommy whispered back. "When he came, I tried to warn him, I said, 'Mr. Mac, I'm afraid you may find a few odd things happening in Castle Keep.' And he looked at me and laughed and he said, 'Och, Tommy, I'm too old to start believing in ghosts.'"

Mr. Maconochie came back, holding a large square rubber-covered flashlight of the kind that can be dropped from a boat without sinking. "Ready for anything," he said, without much conviction.

Jessup said, "Is it always this time of day that the lights go on and off?"

"Any time at all, so long as it's dark. There's no predicting it. That machine has a mind of its own." Mr. Maconochie sighed again, heavily. Then suddenly he stood very still, staring glassily at them all as if he couldn't see them. A strange expression came over his face, a mixture of amazement and dismay. "Of course!" he said. "Of course!"

They looked at him in alarm. "Of course what?" said Jessup.

"I think you'd better come with me," said Mr. Maconochie in an oddly strained voice. Gripping his flashlight, he set off along the corridor, long legs striding, face intent. They hurried after him, with William prancing about and falling under their feet.

Mr. Maconochie led them into the library and switched on all the lights. Immediately the lights went out again. Mr. Maconochie muttered tetchily and switched on his flashlight, sweeping its broad beam across the room toward the MacDevon's big mahogany desk. He crossed to the desk, opened its central drawer, and took out a leather folder.

The lights came on for a count of about three, then went out again, then came back on. Mr. Maconochie sat down on a corner of the desk with the folder on his knee and looked at the children uneasily. "There's something I have to tell you," he said. "But I'm afraid you're going to find it highly unusual and hard to believe. It's about—"

The lights went out again, and in the darkness Tommy lost his patience. "Boggart!" he called irritably. "Will you stop this foolishness! Mr. Mac has something serious he wants to say!"

"It's us, Boggart—Emily and Jessup!" Emily said loudly, happily. "We came all the way from Canada to see you! Are you there, can you hear me?"

Jessup called out, "Please put the lights back on, Boggart! What's the trouble—you don't like the generator?"

The electric lights performed an excited little flicker

of agreement, and then came back on and remained steady.

"That's it!" Tommy said. "He doesn't approve of the electric. Now that's going to be a problem."

Mr. Maconochie had risen from the desk and was standing motionless, stunned, staring at them. *"You know about him!"* he said.

"I should say we do," said Jessup. "We had him in Toronto for months, you wouldn't believe the trouble he caused."

Mr. Maconochie's gaze swiveled to Tommy's face, and became reproachful. "You never *said* you knew!" he said.

"I tried," said Tommy. "You said you were too old to start believing in ghosts."

Mr. Maconochie opened his mouth and shut it again. As if clutching for reality, he resettled his horn-rimmed spectacles on his nose, then took the MacDevon's letter out of his leather folder. "I think you should read this," he said. "I found it in a book about the supernatural."

He handed them the letter. Silently they read it, each in turn, Emily, Jessup, Tommy.

Emily finished reading. She smiled. "He likes peanut butter too," she said.

Jessup finished reading. He said, "It's true that he means no harm. But he sure can cause it if he's in the wrong place."

Tommy finished reading, reached for a handkerchief, and blew his nose in a rather muffled way. "Mr. MacDevon was a fine old man," he said. He handed the letter back to Mr. Maconochie.

Mr. Maconochie said, "Did you and Mr. MacDevon talk about the Boggart?"

"Oh no," Tommy said. "We just both knew we knew, all the time from when I was a wee boy. That's the way you and I will be after a while, Mr. Mac. There's not much to say about the Boggart. He's just there, him and his tricks."

Mr. Maconochie put the leather folder back in the desk. "Thank the Lord they're tricks. Furniture changing from room to room—terrible shrieks at night—I thought I was losing my mind."

"That's what he wanted you to think," Tommy said cheerfully.

Emily laughed aloud. "Oh, I'm so glad he's still here!"

Mr. Maconochie grunted noncommittally. He had retired to Castle Keep in anticipation of a quiet life with no surprises.

Suddenly they became aware of a low, sinister rumbling sound. It was coming from William. He got slowly to his feet and faced the door, tail down, teeth bared, growling ominously. The door swung open, very slowly. William stopped growling, yelped in terror, and tried to hide himself behind Mr. Maconochie's long legs.

In through the door, floating in midair, came a bright blue ski parka that Emily had packed in her duffel bag. It was filled out as it would have been with someone inside it, though it was clearly empty, and its arms were waving merrily as if it were conducting an orchestra. They made a faint swishing sound as the fabric moved through the air.

"Boggart!" cried Emily joyously.

The parka dropped instantly to the ground and lay in a drooping heap. Emily ran to it and stood looking around the room, head up, talking to the air.

"Boggart, it's us, do you remember? We've come back! I told you our great-grandmother was a MacDevon, I told you we'd come back!"

"Hi, Boggart," Jessup said softly. "Greetings from Canada. We missed you."

The lights in the room flickered, but this time did not go out; they grew dim, leaving great caverns of shadow between bookcases and behind armchairs. In one of these patches of dark, they saw a shape begin to grow, glimmering faintly. It had arms, legs, body and head, but it was no recognizable form; tall, thin and ethereal, it hung motionless in the air, a creature of shifting light, nameless, bewitching. Not one of them, afterward, could describe it; they were conscious only of a beauty that caught the breath, of colors shimmering and fading and deepening, as the Northern Lights wonderfully pattern the sky over northern lands.

They gazed in awe at the iridescent, gleaming form, until gradually it began to fade, and while its last echo of shape and color hung in the air they heard a voice, husky, creaky, like an instrument long untuned.

"Tha mo chridhe maille ruibh," it said. *"Tha mo chridhe maille ruibh."*

Then there was silence, and the magic was gone, and the lights in the library rose to their normal brightness.

Emily said, whispering, "What did he say?"

"It's the Gaelic, the line that was at the end of Mr. MacDevon's letter," Tommy said. "It means, *My heart is with you.*"

* * *

EMILY LEANED AGAINST the bathroom doorframe, hugging her dressing gown around her. "Wasn't that marvelous?" she said, still dazed. "Wasn't he just beautiful?" Jessup came out of the bathroom in his pajamas, wiping toothpaste off his chin. "It must be the same as the Aurora Borealis," he said, preoccupied. "Charged particles. Though not in the stratosphere of course. I wish he could explain it to me."

Emily looked at him reproachfully. *"Jess,"* she said.

Jessup grinned. "I know," he said. "I know. No explaining. Just magic."

THREE

THE FOUR OF THEM sat quietly in Mr. Maconochie's sixteen-foot outboard dinghy, bobbing at anchor on the heaving grey-green water of Loch Linnhe. A dozen yards away, waves rose and fell against a bank of glistening seaweed-draped rocks. It was a calm day, with puffs of cloud drifting over a blue sky, but always under these waters lay the echoing rhythm of the swells that rolled toward Appin, around the island of Mull, from the North Atlantic.

Tommy, Emily, Jessup and Mr. Maconochie were gazing at the rocks, waiting. The rocks were called the Seal Rocks, and on and around them the grey Atlantic seals loved to roll and lie when the days were calm. Scotland, like Ireland and Wales, is full of legends about the seal folk, the selkies, who take on the shape sometimes of a human being and sometimes of a seal, and as a result, through generations of tradition, some families have been said to have the blood of seals mixed with the human blood in their veins. The MacDevon family was one of these. And Emily and Jessup belonged to that family, through their father's grandmother, the sister of the last MacDevon, who had emigrated from Scotland to Canada. Emily had never forgotten this; nor had she forgotten the day two years before when on these rocks two seals had surfaced, to gaze at her and at Jessup. "They came up to see you," Tommy had said wonderingly. "I have never known them come so fast, for anyone but Mr. MacDevon."

But no seals emerged today, to roll themselves up onto the kelp-swathed rock, and there was nothing to see, not even for Mr. Maconochie, who sat expectantly holding binoculars, with his long legs bent and his elbows propped on his knees.

"I did see them in the spring," he said hopefully. "Tommy brought me. There was one splendid great fat fellow with barnacles all over his sides."

Emily looked at the empty rocks and found disappointment filling her like an ache; she had felt that the seals, almost as much as the Boggart, were old friends. She said, "Maybe it's just the wrong time of day for—"

Then she stopped. "Oh!" she said, entranced.

Beside the boat, not a yard from where she sat, a shining dark head had emerged, and was gazing at her out of huge long-lashed eyes; a doglike, whiskered head, gleaming, dripping water. It contemplated her for a long moment, then vanished into a wave, and on the other side of the boat Jessup let out a happy yelp as another seal surfaced and stared at him. Then the first was back, and a third, and together the three creatures played around the boat, rising and diving and rolling over in the water, while the children and Mr. Maconochie watched in delight.

Mr. Maconochie said softly, "It's the three daughters of the King of the Sea, come to drop their skins and swim in human form."

"What?" Jessup said.

"Not really," said Mr. Maconochie. "Just an old story."

The first seal surfaced again near Emily, splashing her with water, and as she wiped the spray out of her eyes, laughing, she found a double white cockle shell in her lap.

"Look!" she said to Tommy, still laughing. "He gave me a present!"

She showed him the shell, which was oddly heavy when she picked it up; it seemed to have rock inside it, instead of a cockle. Tommy peered at it.

"That's a fossil shell," he said. "They're special. Did it really come from the seal?"

"It must have done," Emily said.

Tommy gave her an odd, intent look. "Put it in your pocket, and keep it safe," he said.

"Okay," Emily said, and she dutifully put the shell into a pocket of her parka and zipped the pocket shut. The three seals rollicked away through the waves toward the rock, their heads rising and falling, gleaming in the sunlight.

Tommy said, "The Boggart comes to swim with them sometimes. He takes on the shape of a seal, and plays tricks on them."

Jessup squinted at the seals. One of them was hoisting himself up onto the rock, rolling sideways, suddenly bulky and clumsy when out of the sea. He said, "D'you think one of those is the Boggart?"

Tommy shook his head. "You can tell when it's him. Like a good copy, but not quite the real thing. You'll see, soon enough, if the weather holds."

As unexpectedly as they had come, the seals disappeared into the sea. Emily watched them go, through Mr. Maconochie's binoculars. "D'you think it's really true we're related to them?" she said.

"You're a lot slimmer," said Mr. Maconochie.

"And fewer whiskers," Tommy said. He dodged quickly, grinning, as she splashed him.

Mr. Maconochie said, "If the weather does hold—d'you remember I mentioned camping?"

"Yes!" said Jessup promptly.

"Real camping?" said Emily. "With tents and backpacks and all?"

Tommy shook his head. "Mr. Mac is a softie camper," he said. "The gear all gets carried in the car, and the car's right there where you pitch your tent."

Mr. Maconochie said with dignity, "I am an aging man. And who was it chose to sleep *inside* the car, last time?"

"One night in a tent with the dreaded great-nephews was enough," Tommy said. "A frog in my sleeping bag and stones in my sneakers. They're worse than the Boggart." He started the outboard motor. "Pull up the anchor, Jessup."

Emily settled herself contentedly in the bow. "Can

we really go camping? Where shall we go?"

"Almost anywhere," said Mr. Maconochie. "I just want to show you the Highlands. There's more to Western Scotland than Castle Keep."

Jessup dropped the anchor clanking at their feet, and coiled wet line neatly beside it. "Could we go to Loch Ness? Is that far?"

"Certainly we could," said Mr. Maconochie. "Not far at all."

Tommy made a snorting sound, audible even over the chugging of the motor. "Loch Ness! You're surely not thinking of the Monster?"

Jessup frowned. "Why not?"

"That's all tourist rubbish," Tommy said coldly. He nudged the throttle higher, and Jessup sat down suddenly as the boat began to pitch.

"But there was this cool guy on the plane," Jessup said, and all the way home he recited, with much incomprehensible scientific detail, the story of Harold Pindle and his robot submarine expedition. Tommy grunted, unimpressed, and slowed the boat gently down as they came close to Castle Keep's rocky landing.

"That's a classic sound you made," Jessup said. "You've done it twice now. It's the Scornful Scottish Snort."

Tommy's mouth twitched. "When we're by Loch Ness you'll hear another one called the Canny Caledonian Clink. It's the sound of the local Scots collecting money from gullible American monster-hunters."

"I quite liked Harold," Emily said mildly. "And he's Canadian, thank you. He's a professor at the University of British Columbia, and he and Jess talked computers halfway across the Atlantic."

"I bet you didn't tell him about the Boggart," Tommy said.

"Of course not," said Jessup. "He's a scientist. They only believe in things they can see and check and measure. That's what he wants to do to the plesiosaur. If it is a plesiosaur."

Mr. Maconochie stepped out of the dinghy with the bow line as Tommy nudged them up to the rock jetty of the castle. "It's a beautiful loch anyway. Let's dig out the camping gear and you can choose your tents."

So, up in one of the small dark upper rooms of the castle that were used only for storage, they burrowed in numbers of large, exciting boxes ordered by Mr. Maconochie by mail from specialized camping stores. There were tents and sleeping bags, anoraks and boots, packets of improbable freeze-dried food, even shiny blankets of the kind used by astronauts.

"He's like a little kid with those camping catalogs," Tommy told them, pulling out a tent frame so light he could hold it with one finger. "My mum says we should go through his mail and hide them from him. He buys something every month. There's enough stuff up here for an Everest expedition."

"It's the modern materials," Mr. Maconochie said unrepentantly. "They're so amazing, I can never resist them. Look at this!" He pressed lightly on the fragile-looking tent frame, and it sprang open into the inverted bowl shape of a little igloo, bright orange, floor and roof all in one piece, with zippered screens and flaps for windows and doors.

"Look at it! No more hammering tent pegs in the rain, nothing but a quick zip." He zipped up the doorpiece and all the windows, and beamed at them.

Unfortunately he had also zipped up the Boggart, whose limitless curiosity had sent him flittering happily after them into the storage room. Caught in the little tent, he danced about in momentary confusion, and the tent rose into the air like an orange mushroom cap, bouncing off ceiling and walls. The children and Mr. Maconochie were startled only for the first moment; then they grinned, and turned their attention to dodging. "It's a tent, Boggart, not a basketball!" Jessup called cheerfully, ducking as the tent zoomed past his head.

Inside the tent, the Boggart found a gap at the very end of a zipper, and poured himself out through it like water, invisible, greatly relieved. The tent subsided to the floor, and he eyed it resentfully, vowing never to go near anything like it again.

Tommy gingerly unzipped the orange door, and they all waited cautiously to see what the Boggart might do when he came out. But the Boggart was by then already down in the kitchen, sulking a little, sniffing to find out what might be available for supper.

* * *

EVERYTHING THAT HAPPENED afterward could have been traced, perhaps, to Mr. Maconochie's whisky. They had eaten their supper and washed the dishes; Tommy had gone home in his little puttering boat, and now Emily and Jessup sat with Mr. Maconochie beside the fire in the living room, talking about the Boggart's escapades in Toronto two years before. Mr. Maconochie loved hearing about the Boggart. Now that he had discovered the existence of boggarts in general, he felt he had wandered into an entirely different world, whose details he had to learn as a child learns to walk and talk. He was proud of one personal achievement: he had already taught the Boggart to love French fries, known to him and everyone else in the British Isles as chips.

When he retired from the law and moved to Castle Keep, Mr. Maconochie, who in all his life had hardly even boiled an egg, had deliberately set out to learn how to cook. After a long talk with his housekeeper, an elderly, stout Scotswoman who was now herself retiring to live with her niece in Aberdeen, he had persuaded the startled lady to give him lessons in basic cooking. A month later he had a shopping spree in an Edinburgh store frequented mainly by professional chefs, and bought a lifetime supply of shiny pots and pans and ladles and knives. He also accumulated a whole shelf full of cookbooks, which he now read regularly for fun, as most adults read thrillers.

He learned to cook a wide range of dishes, especially those dear to his great-nephews, and he gained six pounds. He was particularly fond of the dinner he had cooked this evening for Emily, Jessup and Tommy: country-style lamb-burgers, made with ground lamb deliciously laced with finely-chopped sautéed onion, green pepper and parsley, accompanied by green peas, with potatoes cut into chips and deep-fried to a wonderful crispness.

Emily and Jessup watched in awe as Mr. Maconochie, wrapped in a white chef's apron, whisked his wire basket of sizzling chips out of the deep fat at precisely the right moment. Their mother, Maggie, had attempted deep-frying only once in recorded history, and they had had to call the fire department because the fat had gone up in flames and set fire to the kitchen curtains.

The Boggart hovered near the table as they ate, and stole chips from each plate in turn with his long invisible fingers. He chewed with lingering pleasure and tried not to burp, and the children tried not to notice whenever a particularly long and delectable chip on one of their plates disappeared. They had experimented with giving the Boggart a plate of his own, but seldom with success. Except on special occasions, he much preferred the trickery of stealing.

Sitting companionably now with them in the living room, curled up in a Japanese cloisonné bowl inherited from Mr. Maconochie's sea-captain grandfather, he drifted in and out of sleep as Jessup regaled Mr. Maconochie with the details of the day the Boggart had put himself into the control system of the traffic lights of Toronto, turning the red lights to blue and causing a variety of traffic accidents. Mr. Maconochie shook his head in concern, and got up to pour himself his evening dram: two fingers' breadth of a good single malt whisky in a graceful round glass.

"Did he understand what he was about?" he asked.

"Oh no," Emily said. "He was just like a kid having fun. I don't think he has a clue of the danger in some of the tricks he plays."

The Boggart paid no attention. All his attention now was on Mr. Maconochie's whisky. A wee dram would be just the thing to set nicely on the fried potatoes, in which perhaps he had overindulged. He flitted across to the table beside Mr. Maconochie's chair, and the next time Mr. Maconochie raised his glass to his lips he found half the whisky had gone.

And so it was Mr. Maconochie's good malt whisky that sent the Boggart flittering a little erratically out of the living room in search of a comfortable bed. Heading for the library, where he rested habitually in a gap on a high shelf, he found himself hovering instead over the pile of camping equipment brought down from the third floor, waiting in the corridor to be loaded the next day into boat and then car.

The Boggart sank downward and landed on a rolled-up blanket, into which he gratefully burrowed and curled up, and fell asleep.

*　　*　　*

SMALL WAVES LAPPED against the stony grey beach of Port Appin, with a gentle rhythmic rasping sound. Emily and Mr. Maconochie left Tommy and Jessup loading bundles from the boat into the Range Rover, and took William across the little graveled parking area to the Camerons' general store.

Tommy's mother came smiling to the door to meet them, smoothing her already smooth and spotless apron, and William bounded toward her, waving his tail and barking joyfully. Though he loved his owner, he was never sorry to be left with the Camerons when Mr. Maconochie went away. He knew it would mean long walks on moors and beaches, instead of the limited space of Castle Keep's island—not to mention the occasional surreptitious treat from the dinner plate of Tommy's father, Angus Cameron, who could never resist a plaintive whine and a hopeful look from large soulful brown eyes.

"Here he is, Mrs. Cameron," said Mr. Maconochie, handing her the basket with William's leash, bowl and favorite blanket. "Seven days' exchange, not very fair— I take away your useful son and leave you my loving but useless dog."

"Not useless at all," said Mrs. Cameron, rubbing William's feathery golden ears. "He makes sure Angus gets some exercise, instead of sitting in the boat or the car all day."

Angus Cameron came out of his storage shed, carrying a large untidy bundle. "I heard that," he said amiably.

Emily gazed at him with interest: he was an exact grown-up version of Tommy, though the curly dark hair had retreated quite a long way up his head. She had never had much contact with Mr. Cameron, a quiet, rather absentminded man who always seemed to be on his way to or from somewhere else. He was a freelance journalist who wrote stories about the Highlands of

Scotland for two or three major British newspapers; it was Mrs. Cameron who very efficiently sold groceries, stamps and almost anything else anyone could need at the village store.

William bounded at Mr. Cameron in happy greeting, and he staggered and put down his bundle. Tommy came from behind Emily and picked it up. "Is this the sleeping bag? Thanks, Dad."

"We bought it for him when we thought he was going to be a Boy Scout," said Mr. Cameron to Emily, fondling William's eager head. "But he only lasted two weeks."

"All the way to Ballachulish to learn to tie knots," said Tommy disdainfully. "You taught me all those knots when I was five years old."

"Well, make sure you tie all the right knots for Mr. Mac," said his mother. "And ring us up a time or two to show you're still breathing. Here's your things." She handed him a bulging backpack, and planted a swift farewell kiss on his cheek before he had a chance to object.

"We'll telephone," said Mr. Maconochie reassuringly. "The first stop is Loch Ness."

"Ah," said Mr. Cameron noncommittally. "Looking for the Monster, are you?"

"*No!*" said Tommy.

Emily said, "Jessup met this professor on the plane who's heading an expedition. He promised to go visit."

"Cool guy," said Jessup, joining them. "He uses laser images from submersibles."

Mr. Cameron said unexpectedly, "You mean Pindle?"

"Yes! Harold Pindle. D'you know him?"

Tommy's father smiled faintly, in the same dismissive way as his son. "I interviewed the man who's hired him—a Swedish millionaire called Axel Kalling."

"What's he like?" said Jessup eagerly.

"A nice man," said Angus Cameron. "Very sweet. And raving mad."

* * *

THIS TIME JESSUP was sitting in the front seat of the Range Rover beside Mr. Maconochie. They were driving along the north shore of Loch Ness, a great grey stretch of water running for miles down the ancient valley that the glaciers of the Ice Age had carved out five thousand years ago. The hills rose purple-brown from the other side of the loch, half a mile away, and gorse bloomed bright yellow and gold along the bank on this side, between the loch and the road. A steamer was moving down the center of the loch, leaving long spreading folds of water behind it.

"Look at the wake of that boat," Tommy said from the back seat. "All you need is a couple of seals to surface in the middle of it, and half a dozen idiots will see a huge swimming monster."

Emily said eagerly, "Are there seals in the loch?"

"Sometimes. But they live in the sea."

The car slowed down, and Mr. Maconochie could be heard muttering under his breath. Ahead of them, a line of vehicles was crawling impatiently behind a large motor-home. They curved slowly around a bend, and a grassy promontory came into view, jutting into the lake, a gentle green against the steely grey water. On it were the unmistakable timeworn half-walls of a ruin.

"There's a castle!" Jessup said.

"Castle Urquhart," Tommy said, as three cars ahead of them pulled into the crowded parking lot above the castle. "Pretty little ruin for tourists to photograph. Very popular on postcards."

Emily looked at the scornful curl of his lip and felt vaguely wounded, as if this were a personal attack. "Well, it *is* pretty," she said rebelliously. "And what's wrong with postcards? Jessup and I are tourists, if it comes to that."

"We are not!" Jessup said with spirit. "Our great-grandmother was a MacDevon."

"We're Canadians and we're visiting," Emily said. "And when Scottish people come to visit Canada, they all go and take photographs of Niagara Falls, and send postcards."

"My auntie did that last year," Tommy said. He grinned at her, and looking at his white teeth and black hair and very blue eyes, Emily felt the hollow feeling in her chest again. She tried to look stern, to cover it up.

Mr. Maconochie made an explosive sound like a cross grunt, and roared past two cars, narrowly missing a tour bus coming at them from the other direction. Turning in her seat, Emily saw Castle Urquhart come into view again behind them on the edge of the loch, its broken grey walls smoothed into mounds by time and the low green grass. She wished they were not leaving it behind quite so fast.

But Mr. Maconochie was hurrying, she found, only because he wanted to be sure they had a place at the campground halfway down Loch Ness. He relaxed, and even pulled off his sweater and rolled up his shirtsleeves, once they were tucked into a corner of the big grassy field overlooking the loch. They set up a small tent for Emily, and a larger one for Mr. Maconochie's lanky frame, and Tommy and Jessup announced their intention of sleeping in the back of the Range Rover, amongst the gear.

"Safe from wandering monsters," said Tommy with a grin.

"Plesiosaurs only eat fish," Jessup said.

"Well, we aren't eating fish, not tonight," said Mr. Maconochie. He busied himself with the ice chest and the supply box in the car while Tommy and Jessup argued about the best way to light a campfire. When they finally had a suitably glowing red mound he fried sausages and bacon and thickly sliced tomatoes in a large frying pan, and served them up with chunks of homemade bread brought from Castle Keep, and what he described as "Vedge." The children looked with grave doubt at Vedge, which turned out to be sprigs of broccoli and cauliflower, small green beans, and chopped red peppers, all precooked but crunchy, cooled and marinated in a dressing of oil, vinegar, brown sugar and mustard. But when they took a first cautious bite they found it so delicious that they gobbled it as fast and thoroughly as the apple pie that followed.

One piece of pie was left on the plate, but everyone had eaten too much to finish it. Mr. Maconochie watched them, beaming indulgently, as if he were their mother. *"Fresh* fruit from now on, not pie," he said. "Campers are supposed to be simple folk."

Deep inside the Range Rover, tucked in his rolled blanket, the Boggart stirred, roused out of his faintly hungover sleep by the alluring smell of frying sausages. When he came flittering hastily out he was infuriated to find nothing left but an empty, greasy frying pan; he never seemed to be in time to encounter sausages, except in their unpleasant naked precooked state. In revenge he gobbled up the last piece of apple pie, and flittered off to the other side of the darkening campground, where a couple of young campers in boots and corduroy shorts were attacking slices of pork pie decorated with ketchup. The Boggart filched a little ketchup, sniffed disdainfully at the pork pie, and floated over the hedge to look down at the loch.

The water lay still and grey in the dying light, unruffled now by any boat or bird. House lights were beginning to glimmer far away on the other side, like little stars prickling the dark mass of trees.

And then the Boggart was suddenly stopped, as if he had flown into an invisible wall.

He dropped down onto the branch of a tree and sat there, very still. Something most unexpected, something long forgotten, was beginning to happen inside his head. He could feel his senses quivering, calling deep inside him to the few very faint memories that lie far back and neglected in a boggart mind. What were they trying to say to him? He tried hard to concentrate: *What is it? What is it?*

Somehow he knew this place . . . there was somebody in this place that he had known, a long time ago, long ago in the beginning of things . . . Someone he had known as well as a brother, someone close . . . cousin, cuz . . . cousin, cuz . . . Someone of whom he had heard no word or hint for years, for decades, for centuries . . . someone . . . cousin . . . cuz . . . .

He shot upward suddenly into the sky, astonishing a dozing owl and a dozen busy swallows. "*Nessie!*" he cried joyfully, in the ancient language of boggarts. "*Nessie! Where are you? It's me, it's your cuz!*"

Over the loch he swooped and darted, excited, rediscovering, feeling deep in his misty mind the stirrings of a huge affection he had forgotten long ago. He called and he called, happily, imploringly.

And down at the bottom of the loch, seven hundred feet down in the mud and the slime, his boggart cousin Nessie stirred. He shifted his huge bulk, just a little, hearing a dim echo of a voice he had not heard for hundreds of years. But he was deep, deep asleep, without ever having moved so much as a muscle for a decade, and the call was not loud enough nor near enough to reach his fuddled brain.

Nessie lifted his head a fraction of an inch, just enough to stir the mud and to cloud the deep, cold water a very little. He heard nothing. He dropped again into stillness, and went back to sleep.

FOUR

✳

ALL NIGHT the Boggart flittered restlessly to and fro, over the shores and the silent water of Loch Ness. His passing blurred the radar of the local bats, as they swooped low, hunting for mosquitoes, and they scolded him in tiny piping voices. He paid no attention; he was unsettled, caught in a mist of unaccustomed emotion. What was happening to him? For an unattached, carefree creature like a boggart, it was strange to feel anything more intense than a faint twitch of greed—and what he was feeling now was a deep, ancient ache, the longing for family. He whimpered softly to himself, knowing without comprehension that suddenly he felt incomplete.

He flittered over the dark water, disconsolate, while the moon gradually rose and fell and the bright stars prickled the sky. He called to his cousin, or the thought of his cousin, sometimes aloud and sometimes in the silent speech of the Old Things.

But still, at the bottom of the loch, Nessie slept on.

* * *

Jessup woke at first light, sat bolt upright, and banged his head on the roof of the Range Rover. His startled yelp woke Tommy, who rolled over and stared owlishly at him out of his sleeping bag.

"Sorry," Jessup said.

Tommy yawned, and tried to push his tousled black hair out of his eyes. "Now if we'd slept in a tent, you'd not be hitting your head."

"I was dreaming. I was in one of Harold's submersibles, and there was this huge white shark, like in 'Jaws.' Up against the window, all teeth, trying to bite the glass."

"I thought you said those submersible things didn't carry people."

"They don't. It was a *dream,* Tommy."

"I like the shark," Tommy said. "It could help us cut down on visitors." He wriggled out of his sleeping bag and began hastily pulling on his clothes. Jessup suddenly realized how cold he was feeling, and did the same.

"It's freezing! And it's August!"

"You're in Scotland," Tommy said without sympathy. "A country for men." He rubbed a hole in the mist on the car window, and looked out. "And boggarts."

Jessup rubbed a hole of his own, and saw twigs and sticks of kindling arranging themselves over the dead ashes of the campfire. Two small logs rose into the air and perched on top of the sticks. A large matchbox hovered nearby and opened, and a match jumped out and struck itself on the side of the box. Flaming, it moved gently downward and set light to the twigs. The twigs flared up, as did the kindling, and one side of the little fire glowed brighter than the rest, as if someone were blowing on it.

Jessup watched, entranced. "Cool!"

Tommy scrambled over the back of the driver's seat and pressed the button to open the tailgate window. "Not so cool if anyone else sees him." He scrambled back again, dropped the tailgate, and sat on the edge, peering around the campsite. But nobody was stirring nearby: only a tall blond couple on the other side of the field, busily folding up their tent.

Jessup pulled on his sneakers and a second sweater, and prepared to tiptoe to Emily's small round tent and make hideous plesiosaur noises outside. But a movement caught his eye, and he looked up. He froze.

The water bucket, from which they had filled kettle and washbowls last night, had been left empty outside Mr. Maconochie's tent. Suddenly now it rose into the air, and began moving briskly across the campground toward the standpipe from which all campers drew their water. Suspended about eighteen inches from the ground, it made a beeline for the faucet: an impossible sight, an empty bucket, flying. And Jessup saw that to reach the standpipe, it would have to pass the two blond campers folding up their tent.

Appalled, he opened his mouth to yell after the invisible Boggart, but promptly shut it again. If the campers heard him shout, they would look up—and see the flying bucket. Jessup took off across the field, running as fast as he could—not directly after the Boggart, but in a wide curve that would take him to the other side of the campers' field of vision. Tommy watched him in astonishment.

Jessup came tearing across the grass to the two strangers, and skidded to a halt, smiling a big false smile at them. "Can I help?" he said brightly.

They stared at him blankly: two very large young people, a man and a woman, with pale skin and hair so fair it was almost white. They wore shorts and boots, and fuzzy Fair Isle sweaters. "Excuse?" said the young man politely.

"Uh—I wondered if I could help you pack," Jessup said. Over the young woman's shoulder he saw the bucket float merrily past on its way to the standpipe. He smiled even wider, gazing up into her puzzled blue eyes. "Help?" he said, beaming idiotically. He noticed that the tent was now neatly folded, waiting to go into one of their two bulging backpacks. Everything else was clearly already packed. Still desperately smiling, Jessup seized the tent, and tried to stuff it into the backpack.

"*Nein, nein!*" said the young man indignantly. He ripped the tent out of Jessup's hands and turned to two sturdy bicycles which, Jessup now saw, were waiting beside the hedge. Their panniers were laden, but in one pannier there was still a neat tent-sized space. The young man fitted in the tent, and gave Jessup a wary, unsmiling nod.

"Ah," Jessup said weakly. In the background he saw the bucket descend to the ground underneath the stand-pipe. The faucet turned, in the Boggart's invisible fingers, and water began to gush loudly down. As the two blond heads began to turn, Jessup let out a shrill cackling laugh. The heads snapped back in alarm, and the young woman shot her partner a quick look and swung her backpack up onto her shoulders. The man did the same, and Jessup gave his backpack a helpful push. Over his shoulder he could see that Tommy had come running up to the standpipe, so that the bucket no longer seemed to be self-propelled.

"Danke schon," said the blonde young woman to Jessup, retreating nervously to her bicycle. "Dank you very moch."

The young man ducked his head stiffly in Jessup's direction, and the two of them climbed rapidly onto their bicycles and rode away, bumping uncomfortably over the grass. Jessup saw them looking uncertainly back at him from the gate of the field, as he crossed to join Tommy and the bucket.

"Boggart," Tommy was saying reprovingly to the air in the general region of the bucket, "we all have a great time with your tricks, but they're not such a good idea with strangers around."

From somewhere in the field close by them, a strange, creaky voice spoke; the same husky, whispering voice that they had heard in the library of Castle Keep.

"Is fada fuar an oidhche a bh'ann," it said. *"Tha feum oirnn cupan teatha gasda teth."*

There was silence again, except for the gulls crying faintly, out over the loch.

"He's talking again!" Jessup said softly. "It's amazing! He never used to do that. That's Gaelic, isn't it? What did he say?"

Tommy was grinning. He picked up the brimming bucket of water. "It wasn't a game, just for once. He says it was a long cold night. He says we need water for a nice hot cup of tea."

* * *

THEY CAME BLINKING out into the daylight from the Loch Ness Tourist Centre, where films and photographs and models had given them an exhaustive survey of the sightings of the Loch Ness Monster. Before them, the road ran along the length of the loch; the water glinted under patchy sunshine. Tommy had a handful of leaflets, and was peering at them crossly.

"Lot of rubbish," he said, scowling.

"It does seem to me," said Mr. Maconochie mildly, "that there was a remarkably long gap between St. Columba seeing a monster in the year five sixty-five A.D., and all those reports of sightings in the early nineteen-thirties."

"But that was just the newspapers," Jessup said. "People have been seeing monsters for centuries, there just weren't any papers to write about them."

"Monsters?" said Emily. "Plural?"

"Harold says there's a family. And there must be, because one single creature could never have survived this long. The parent plesiosaur dies, and then people see the next generation and think it's the same one."

Tommy waved a leaflet at him. "This was the only plesiosaur picture, right? The famous one, with the long neck? And then in nineteen ninety-one the man who took it confessed he'd really photographed a model, made from plastic wood stuck on a toy submarine from Woolworth. Just another hoax!"

Emily looked at him unhappily. His Scottish accent was suddenly very marked, and his blue eyes bright with passionate disbelief. She was not accustomed to having her brother and Tommy furiously disagree; it made her nervous.

"You need to meet Harold," Jessup said obstinately.

They all turned to look at the long windowless rectangular building set in the parking lot beside the Tourist Centre. It was labeled "Kalling-Pindle Research Project," and it had been locked and silent when they arrived. Now, a big door at one end stood open, with a four-step stairway jutting down from it, and a bicycle was leaning against its wall.

Jessup ran over to the open door. "Harold?" he called. But there was no answer from inside.

The Boggart rose from his comfortable seat on Mr. Maconochie's broad, unwitting shoulder, and flittered in through the trailer door. He found a jungle of wires and small glowing screens, in a narrow corridor that linked three spaces like small rooms. Each room held a desk with a bank of instruments and larger screens. Venturing into the third and furthest room, he bumped into a chunky young man wearing shorts, a black T-shirt with the sleeves torn off, and earphones. The black T-shirt was decorated across the chest in large white letters with the words MEAN MAN.

The young man spluttered, and wiped a hand over his face as if brushing off a cobweb. Caught unawares, the Boggart rolled head over heels in the air and reeled giddily back down the little corridor, passing Jessup, who was now standing inside the trailer calling tentatively, "Harold?"

"Harold's not here," said the young man, firmly blocking Jessup's way. He had a nasal American accent, and a rather high voice in spite of the bulging biceps revealed by the torn-off sleeves. He looked down past Jessup at Tommy, Emily and Mr. Maconochie. "This trailer's private," he added.

The Boggart flittered upward and sat in a tree. He watched the muscular young man with an unfriendly eye.

Jessup backed down the stairs. "I'm sorry," he said. "But Harold asked me to come visit. My name's Jessup Volnik."

"It's still private, whatever your name is," said Mean Man. "Come back tomorrow. Or next week." He pulled a wire mesh screen down over the end of the trailer, and let it drop with a crash. Then he disappeared into the depths behind it.

But a truck came swinging into the parking lot from the road that ran along the lake: a noisy little pickup with a large plastic-swathed piece of machinery in the back. Out of the cab jumped Harold Pindle, still in the sweatshirt and jeans he had worn on the airplane. "Jessup!" he cried. "Emily! Welcome!"

He reached out remarkably long arms, like an octo-pus, hugging them both as if he had known them since birth. Then he shook hands enthusiastically with Tommy and Mr. Maconochie. "You're Mr. Mac! The lawyer who bought a castle! And Tommy the computer whiz! Come on all of you and meet Jenny, and Adelaide!"

Jenny, climbing out of the pickup's cab with an armful of papers, turned out to be Harold's assistant: a small, tough-looking Chinese-American girl with a black ponytail and a cheerful, ready smile. Adelaide was the machine wrapped in plastic: a Remotely Operated Vehicle, known as an ROV. She was the size of a dining-room table, rectangular, with a bright yellow tubular frame and casing and a great many cables and dials and wires. Jenny unwrapped the plastic to show her off, and Harold patted the yellow frame affectionately.

"This is one of the two babies who are going to help us find the Monster," he said. "Sweet Adelaide, down she goes under the water tomorrow to join her brother— and *then* we'll see!"

"What's the other one called?" said Emily.

"Sydney," said Jenny. "Harold was born in Australia."

"Sydney and Adelaide between them will scour the loch," said Harold with satisfaction. "And it won't just be side-scan sonar—we'll have a laser line scan. There's only about half a dozen of those in the world. Amazing business—it converts to color pictures just like your TV set. Come on in and see."

He leaped up the trailer steps and rattled the wire mesh screen. "Chuck!" he bellowed. "Open up!"

Mean Man appeared out of the darkness, looked at them all in silence, and reluctantly unlocked the barrier. He instantly vanished again into the depths.

"Chuck doesn't like people," said Harold cheerfully. "He prefers Sydney and Adelaide. But he's a very good technician. Come on in."

They climbed the little ladder after him, with the Boggart in pursuit, and squeezed into the spaces between equipment in the trailer. Mr. Maconochie found a coil of wire jutting into his neck, and tried to make himself shorter.

Harold tugged the wire out of Mr. Maconochie's collar. "Not much room, I'm afraid," he said. "This thing's really a container. Had it shipped over just like this, full of the equipment and a lot of plastic packing. A truck brought it here, and all we had to do was open the door, pull out the packing, plug in, and set up shop."

Head slightly bent, Mr. Maconochie looked around in wonder at the array of dials and gauges and switches. It looked like the control room of a nuclear submarine. He said, "This must have cost a small fortune."

Harold Pindle chuckled. "Sure did. We have an angel. A wonderful old fellow called Axel Kalling, of Kalling Match—he has a foundation that supports unfashionable scientific enterprises. Like mine . . . Now take a look at this, Jessup—"

He sat down at a control panel in front of what looked like a television screen and began turning dials, and a hazy image appeared at the top of the screen, obscured by a thick brown fog.

Emily peered over his shoulder. "It looks like the bottom of a boat."

"That's just what it is," said Harold.

Jessup said, "That's the straight visual image, right?"

"Right. This is from a video camera mounted on Sydney's bow, with lights of course. Cousteau stuff, just like on the box. But in here we have the sonar—stage two." Harold bounced up again and into the next cavelike space in the wire-draped trailer, and Jessup, Emily and Mr. Maconochie dutifully followed, ducking cautiously.

The Boggart was bored. Screens and computer terminals had lost most of their charm for him once he had learned how to play tricks with them, and these days he seldom even bothered to send Disney cartoons invading Mr. Maconochie's favorite BBC television dramas. He flittered out of the trailer, back into the daylight; across the asphalt of the parking lot and over the litter bin into which Tommy had scornfully dropped his Loch Ness Monster leaflets.

Glancing down, he saw on the front of a discarded leaflet the fuzzy, fake, world-famous picture of the Monster: the plesiosaur form rearing out of the water, with its massive body, long neck and tiny head. The Boggart paused, and all his yearnings of the long melancholy night came flooding back. He looked across the road to the loch, wide and silent and grey under the clouded sky, and he launched himself toward the water with all his ancient senses alert.

"*Cuz!*" he cried. "*Cuz, where are you? It's me!*"

Seven hundred feet down in the frigid dark water, the echo of the Boggart's voice crept into Nessie's sleeping brain. He shook his head a little, preparing to go deeper down into sleep, but the voice would not go away. It rang in his brain, louder, clearer, and Nessie gave a small grumbling grunt and raised his head. A layer of mud ten years thick rose with it, and wafted out into the water, which had been unclouded since the last time Nessie had floated lazily to the surface, peered out at a startled tourist, drifted down again before any camera could click, and gone back to sleep.

"*Nessie! Where are you? It's your cuz, it's me!*"

Suddenly Nessie's senses leaped into life, fighting their way to wakefulness through his long habit of sleep. He knew that voice. He had known it well, oh very well indeed, years and centuries ago. A great excitement came flooding through him. He lifted his long neck and shook his enormous body free of the mud, and with a beat of his powerful tail he was on his way up to the surface, calling as he went even though hundreds of feet of water kept his voice from being heard.

"*Cuz! It's me, it's Nessie! I'm coming! Wait for me!*"

*　*　*

UP IN THE TRAILER, Harold had shown them his sonar screens, and now he had reached the third set of equipment, in the last little cave at the very back. Here there were banks of dials and computer keyboards, and three small screens in a row, each a blank dark green. There was so little space that Emily, Jessup and Mr. Maconochie had to take turns to peek inside, and even Harold had to stand squeezed at the back while Chuck, morose and silent in his Mean Man T-shirt, sat at the ROV remote controls that only he could fully understand.

"This laser scan is quite amazing," Harold said happily. "Nobody's had it before. We can send Sydney off through that deep dark water with no lights, and no sound waves for sonar, and if he meets anything we can get a picture of it as clear as if he was shooting with a video camera in daylight. Chuck, is Jenny out there with Sydney?"

Chuck looked at them all disapprovingly, clearly wishing they would go away. "She's in the other boat, making it ready for Adelaide," he said.

"Well, tell her to move to Sydney's boat and cast off for a little bit," Harold said.

Chuck breathed heavily, and murmured into the little microphone attached to his headset. Then he played with his dials, and after a while the three little screens faded to a lighter green and occasional pictures began to appear on them, dark and distinct: a mooring line, the side of a jetty, an anchor, moving upward.

"They're out in the loch," Chuck said. He glowered at Harold; his expression said, *You're wasting valuable scientific time showing off to strangers.* He added, "Jenny's turning north."

Then he looked more closely at his dials, and from the dials to the screens and back, and his face changed. He began to blink very fast, and he said huskily, "There's something moving out there, underwater. Something very big."

*　*　*

NESSIE SHOT THROUGH the darkness, flippers and tail churning, thrusting him upward; all the mud and slime fell away from him as he rushed through the water. He was calling all the while to the Boggart as he came, and above him the Boggart hovered invisible over the loch, hearing, ecstatic, waiting for him to arrive.

"Nessie! Is it really you?"

"I'm coming, cuz! Wait for me! I'm on my way!"

Impatiently the Boggart waited, wondering what was taking so long; boggart-travel, for a creature of no substance or tangible form, was a matter of seconds when you put your mind to it. Well, Nessie had always been a slowpoke. Looking down, he saw below him one of the long, sturdy research boats of the Kalling-Pindle Project putting out into the loch, with Jenny at the helm. Then beyond it, to his horror, he saw fast approaching him the telltale ripple of a speeding underwater form—a very large form. Nessie was still in the shape of the Monster.

The Boggart was appalled.

"Nessie! What's the matter with you? Drop your shape! You're a boggart, man!"

Nessie slowed down, feeling a slow shame. *"I cannae do it! I've forgotten how!"*

"You can't forget how!" the Boggart howled. *"Go to invisible! Or something smaller!"*

Nessie's massive form continued to rush toward him through the water, driven by the broad powerful flippers, driven by longing. He was visible on the surface now, leaving a magnificent wake, the sinuous curve of his great back gleaming above the foaming surface. From the research boat below him the Boggart heard a muffled shriek. He bellowed frantically at Nessie again.

"Change your shape!"

"I cannae do it! Help me!"

The Boggart groaned, and tried to remember things he had learned so many centuries ago that they were part of the unthinking shape of his mind. In the Old Speech without words he shouted ancient instructions to Nessie: how to find the shapes that can take all shape away, how to use the imagination that can change all images, how to disappear.

Nessie heard and desperately tried to obey, flailing closer all the time to the Boggart and to the boat. But he was still his massive self, solid and vast and amazing, and visible.

"I cannae do it! I cannae!"

* * *

IN THE TRAILER they stared at the screens, as Chuck

hunched over his control panel and played with the
dials like a pianist caressing his piano keys. Emily
could hear Jessup breathing fast at her side, and she
felt Tommy tense just behind her. She thrust her
hands convulsively into her pockets, and her fingers
met the little fossil shell she had left there on a calmer
day. It seemed to push itself into her palm, as if with
a force of its own. Harold leaned forward, oblivious to
everything but the screens.

And gradually in each of the three green squares
they saw an image appear and grow, an image familiar
and unmistakable even though none of them had ever
seen it live before. There coming toward them was the
Loch Ness Monster, long neck extended, legs back,
driven by its long powerful tail, swimming through
the loch. Closer and closer it came, more and more
vivid.

Tommy grasped Emily's shoulders in excitement.
Jessup cheered. Harold shouted with delight, and
banged on the back of a chair like a happy little boy.
"Go to video!" he yelled. "Quick, quick!"

"It's him!" Chuck whispered hoarsely. "It's him!"

His fingers worked furiously on the controls, and
in a close-up as clear as a television newsreel they saw
the great grey-green neck rearing up over them, and
above it the head, jaws open and dripping, gazing at
the sky. Instinctively they flinched backward.
Tommy's fingers tightened on Emily's shoulders;
Emily's fingers clutched her shell, turning it over and
over, like a talisman.

Then suddenly, in an instant, the Monster disappeared.

* * *

UNDER THE LOCH, two boggarts whirled about each other, in delight and relief.

"*Well done, Nessie! I knew you could do it!*"

"*Oh cuz! I'm so glad to find you, cuz!*"

FIVE

✳

HAROLD YELPED in frustration. "It's dived! Go back to laser scan!"

Chuck was already punching buttons and turning dials, cursing under his breath. There was a dark patch of sweat on the back of his T-shirt. But all the screens were blank.

Harold seized a microphone. "Jenny!" he called urgently. "Where is it? Where did it go?"

Emily was suddenly vividly aware of Tommy's hands clutching her shoulders. She sat very still. Tommy didn't let go, but he slackened his grip; his fingers moved a little as if he were giving her a neck-rub. Emily thought she had never felt anything more magical in her life.

"It was Nessie," Tommy said softly, marveling. "Nessie's real."

Jenny's voice came over the intercom, baffled, high with strain. "It was here! It was huge, right over us, dripping, I could smell it—and then it wasn't here any more."

Mr. Maconochie said softly, "A very ancient and a fishlike smell."

Jenny had heard him. "That's right—how did you know?" said her voice on the intercom.

"That was another monster," Mr. Maconochie said. "Called Caliban."

Jessup was making a quiet crowing sound. He looked around at Tommy. "Well?" he said. "Well?"

"All right," Tommy said. "You told me so."

Harold and Chuck were on their feet, heading for the next cave of equipment. Buzzers were sounding, lights were flashing; the trailer was suddenly too full of people. "Folks," Harold said, "I'm sorry, but—"

"We're gone," Jessup said. "Till tomorrow." They ducked out of the way, hastily. Jessup thumped Harold on the back as he left, and Harold flashed them the grin of a happy, fulfilled, joyous man.

* * *

THE BOGGART SAID SEVERELY, in the formless, telepathic Old Speech, *"This is not proper behavior, for a boggart. We are shape-shifters, not monsters or trolls."*

"Don't be cross with me, cuz. It's been so long, and I never was good at shifting anyway." Nessie looked down in delight at the small waves along the shore, as they flittered together over the loch. *"Oh it's so good to be with you— and up in the air!"* He turned a happy aerial somersault.

The Boggart twirled after him. *"It is so! And now you can stay as you should be, and we'll have a grand time all up and down the lochs. Just like the old days."*

Nessie said doubtfully, *"We can try. But I've lived in the one shape for so long now—sooner or later I'll slip back into it, you know. I surely will when I fall asleep."*

"Think yourself out of it. I'll help you."

"It's hard," Nessie said plaintively. He sneezed, as a seagull flew through him. *"It's very hard."*

* * *

AFTER SUPPER THAT NIGHT, Mr. Maconochie and the children sat at the edge of the campground, overlooking the loch. The sky was clouded now, the air chill, and they were huddled into sweaters and parkas. The water lay lead-colored, still and sinister, rippled only by the wake of an occasional small boat.

Emily said, bemused, "We've seen the Loch Ness Monster."

Jessup was staring at the loch through binoculars. "We sure have!" he said happily.

"Maybe it'll be on TV tonight," Tommy said. "We should have tried the car radio."

"That depends how many other people saw it," Mr. Maconochie said. His voice was quiet and neutral, but something in it turned their heads to look at him.

Jessup said, "What d'you mean, Mr. Mac?"

"We saw an *image* of the Loch Ness Monster," Mr. Maconochie said. "On a screen. We did not see the creature live, in the flesh."

"Jenny did," Emily said. "And smelled him too."

"And then it disappeared," Mr. Maconochie said.

"Well, yes—but we *saw* him."

"Your friend Professor Pindle said it dived. Did you see it dive?"

"No," Tommy said thoughtfully. "It just vanished off the screen."

Jessup put down his glasses and looked searchingly at Mr. Maconochie. "What are you suggesting, Mr. Mac?"

Mr. Maconochie rubbed his neck, looking perplexed. "I don't really know. It just seems to me that the only way a real solid creature disappears is by going somewhere else. But an image on a screen can disappear instantly by being switched off."

"He *wasn't* an image!" Emily said plaintively. "He wasn't switched off!"

"D'you think this has anything to do with the Boggart?" Tommy said.

"Of course not," Jessup said firmly. "A plesiosaur may be amazing but it's not magic."

Emily said, more loudly, "You're wrong, Mr. Mac! Jenny *saw* him!"

Tommy patted her hand. "Maybe we should talk to Jenny. What do you think, Jessup?"

"I think we should go make some hot chocolate," Jessup said.

* * *

THE BOGGART WAS not in good enough spirits to steal anyone's hot chocolate beside the little campfire that night. He sat morosely on top of the Range Rover, brooding. He had already lost Nessie again, for the time being. For a while it had been wonderful; they had thought of nothing but the delight of finding each other again. They had flittered and laughed and talked and sung, and each of them had been happier than they ever remembered.

Then they had dived down together into the cold deep water that had been Nessie's home for so long, and in the flicker of an eye the Boggart had taken the shape of a seal, as he so often did when he found himself swimming. But Nessie remained his insubstantial boggart-self, with the weeds and water slipping through him.

"Come on, Nessie—be a selkie, the way we always did!" The Boggart rolled and turned and somersaulted in the water, playful, beckoning. Nessie moaned softly, and hovered motionless, a faint flickering presence, iridescent, glowing. A passing salmon, sensing him, moved politely out of the way.

"Nessie! Come on!"

"I told you, I cannae do the changing any more! I'm weary!"

And in an instant Nessie dropped into sudden sleep, as boggarts often will—and changed at once into his immense Monster-shape. The Boggart watched in despair as the huge body drifted down, down to the icy depths of the loch, there to lie sleeping deep and long on his mattress of mud.

There Nessie still lay now, while the Boggart perched on the roof of the Range Rover, and the night

grew black all around. Tommy and Jessup slept peacefully inside the car, and Emily and Mr. Maconochie in
their tents. The clouds blew apart a little, to show a
gleaming sliver of moon, and two of the bright stars of
the Plough. The Boggart sighed, heartrendingly, and
from a scrub oak nearby a barn owl hooted to him in
reply. The clouds drifted over the moon again, and the
night was dark.

Down through the gap left open at the top of the
window, the Boggart poured himself like water into the
back of the Range Rover, where the two boys lay
wrapped in their sleeping bags, two cloth-covered
cocoons. He hovered over them, feeling a great longing
to share the troublesome mixture of emotion that was
whirling through him: the worries, the love of kin, the
memories that came so seldom but would not now go
away. His thoughts flew into and through Tommy's
sleeping mind, like music waiting to be heard. But
Tommy was dreaming of Emily, dancing a Scottish reel
with her in his sleep, and could not hear him.

The Boggart too thought of Emily, but Emily was
out in that difficult orange mushroom of a tent, which
he had sworn not to go near. So instead he hovered
over the head he had felt was least likely to pick up his
plaintive signals: the head of Jessup, whose rational bril-
liance was quite likely to provide a barrier to the flickering whispers of an Old Thing.

But there was no barrier. And Jessup began to dream.

He was an observer, in his dream, suspended somehow in the air, over the waves of Loch Linnhe. He was

far in the past, he knew, for even though this was certainly Loch Linnhe, backed by the outline of Lismore Island and the faint blue hills of the Isle of Mull, there was no sign of Castle Keep. There was only the bare rock on which, in the thirteenth century, the castle would be built. Grass and some scrubby bushes grew on the rock, and the waves lapped its edges—and in the waves, two glowing formless creatures magically played.

Smiling in his dream, Jessup watched the flicker and flash of light as the creatures twisted and danced in the water, and he knew that they were boggarts. He had seen that kind of wonderful iridescence only once in his life, when the Boggart had shown himself to them in the MacDevon's library. As he watched, the boggarts darted through the waves to the Seal Rocks, and the grey seals, looking just as they did in the present day, splashed into the water and joined the swift, playful game that was a dance. Dreaming, Jessup knew that this was a dream, and longed for it not to end.

He saw Castle Keep then, rearing up on the rock, its stones magically bright and new-cut as they were when it was first built. He found himself inside the castle, its walls hung with tapestries and lit by smoking torches, and he saw human figures, though only vaguely, and knew that the Boggart was there, attached to Castle Keep now, playing his tricks. These people must be the first MacDevons, the beginning of the family with which the Boggart had lived for so many centuries, in this one home. He wondered where the other boggart had gone.

And the instant that the thought came into his sleeping head, he found himself on the ramparts of another castle, bigger and more elaborate, overlooking a loch and forested mountains. Beside him he saw two children, younger than himself, laughing as water poured into a bowl from a jug held by disembodied hands—and he knew that this was the place to which the other boggart had attached himself, and this the family. Looking out across the water, he realized that the loch was Loch Ness. So the castle must be Castle Urquhart, which he in the twentieth century had seen only as a ruin of tumbled stones and grass.

Jessup was overwhelmed by an immensely strong sense of home, of belonging, and knew that he was feeling what the two boggarts felt for their respective castles and people, through the years. He saw the passing of the centuries, as if pages were flicking before him and carrying the castle with them; he saw other children, in other times, and saw the Loch Ness boggart changing his shape for them: from a little black cat to a long white snake, to a four-tined stag, to a unicorn. And then, to a huge grey-bodied monster swimming in the loch, with a long neck and a small bright-eyed head. . . .

In the moment that he recognized the image, from his space somewhere in the air he heard a great terrible noise, and saw Castle Urquhart explode into a sudden immense burst of smoke and flame, with stone and wood flying out in blazing arcs and into the loch. Jessup shouted in horror.

And then he woke up.

Tommy was leaning over him, gazing down at him in concern. "Jessup! You having a nightmare? Are you okay?"

Jessup blinked at him, trying to remember where he was. "Uh," he said. "Ah. Uh."

There was a tapping at the rear window and Tommy saw Emily's face, pale and concerned; he unrolled the window to let her in. "Jessup was dreaming," he said.

Emily said, "I thought one of you was being murdered."

"Somebody blew up the castle," Jessup said.

Emily stared at him. "What castle?"

"Castle Urquhart, the one that's a ruin. They blew it up, and he got stuck in the shape he was playing in. And he was so lonely after that, he just slept and slept for hundreds of years."

Emily rolled her eyes at Tommy, and tugged her parka tighter around her pajamas. "He's still dreaming," she said.

"I'm not, I'm awake, I'm awake!" Jessup sat upright, and banged his head on the car roof again.

"Oh *Jess!*" said Emily. She reached out maternally to feel his head.

Jessup shook her hand away ungratefully. He said, "He was lonely, don't you see? He just didn't enjoy being awake. That's why he slept for so long."

"Why *who* slept so long?"

"The Loch Ness Monster," Jessup said. "Only he's not a monster and he's not a plesiosaur. He's a boggart."

"A *boggart?*"

"Just like ours. But . . . clumsier."

Emily looked at him sympathetically. "This was quite some dream. It must have been the fish and chips. We'll talk about it in the morning." She scrambled down off the tailgate, into the shadowy night.

"Wait a minute, Em," Tommy said. He reached out, as she paused, and took her hand. Emily stood still, and looked at him sideways.

"Remember when the Monster disappeared, while we were looking at him on Harold's screen?" Tommy said. "Remember Mr. Mac saying he couldn't really have been there, because no real creature could disappear like that?"

"Mmm," said Emily uncertainly.

"Well, he could too have disappeared—if he were a boggart. Our Boggart does."

Emily nodded slowly, as a dozen swift images of the shape-shifting Boggart danced around her memory. She looked around at the dark campground and the night sky. "He came with us, our Boggart, didn't he? Where d'you suppose he's been today?"

"I think he's been giving Jessup a dream," Tommy said.

In the air around them, so faint and diffuse that they couldn't tell if it were inside the car or part of the night itself, they heard a low sound growing, a low warm sound, lapping them with approval, like the purring of a cat.

SIX

✳

Jessup said, "And in the minute after the castle exploded, when I was waking up, I had this terrible feeling of how lonely he was. Lonely, lonely, down in that dark water. And I really wanted to do something about it."

He was sitting beside Mr. Maconochie, looking out at the loch as they drove toward Harold Pindle's trailer. The long gleaming expanse of water stretched beside and before them, and now and then as the road curved they could see the grey-green mound of the ruined Castle Urquhart in the distance.

Tommy said, "That was what the Boggart was putting into your head. His own feelings. He hates Nessie being lonely."

"And he wants to do something about it," Emily said. Their two earnest heads leaned forward from the back seat, into the gap between Jessup and Mr. Maconochie.

"Nnnnnnnn," said Mr. Maconochie. It was a kind of growling hum, full of uncertainty.

Jessup looked at him accusingly. "You don't believe me!"

"Jessup," Mr. Maconochie said. "I believe in your dream and I certainly believe in your Boggart—our Boggart. It just seems to me that the dream must have come from your imagination."

"Maybe he'll give *you* a dream," Emily said.

Tommy shook his head. "No. Mr. Mac would just think his own imagination was making it up."

Mr. Maconochie turned into the little gravel-topped parking area beside the long metallic rectangle of the Kalling-Pindle Project. "Oh dear," he said. "Boggarts and monsters and messages in dreams. This is a sore test for an elderly member of the legal profession."

"The Boggart has to find special ways of talking to us," Emily said insistently. "He always has. He's very bad at spoken words, he can only manage a few at a time."

Jessup had fallen silent. He was looking at Harold Pindle, who was coming down the steps of the research trailer with a stranger, a small man with a lot of white hair. "What do we do about Harold?" he said glumly. "He's so set on proving Nessie is a plesiosaur. What's he going to do when he finds it's not true?"

* * *

THE BOGGART WAS SLOWLY circling Nessie's massive sleeping body, like an invisible coronet of floating weed. *"Nessie, wake up. Come on now, you're not really asleep, you've had enough sleep for sixteen boggarts, these last few centuries."*

Nessie opened one eye and regarded him mournfully. *"They blew up my castle,"* he said. *"My family went away."*

"That was three hundred years ago!" the Boggart said. *"And anyway I'm your family."*

"You are. I'm sorry, cuz." Penitent, Nessie raised his long neck and, with a huge effort, tried to shift his shape from solid monster to insubstantial boggart. It took great effort, and he was lamentably out of practice. First he shrank to a thin monster, like a large aquatic giraffe; then a very small one, like a plastic dinosaur from a cereal package. At last he managed to dwindle completely away, reappearing—to the Boggart at least—as the iridescent flicker of energy that was his natural invisible form.

They turned somersaults around each other in the murky water, and the whirling current made by their somersaults rose to the surface and completely turned around the little boat in which Jenny, wearing a baseball cap, was sculling across the lake. Jenny had rowed in the MIT lightweight women's crew when she was a student, and liked to keep in practice wherever she was. She rested on her oars and stared in astonishment at the wooded shore of the lake, which she had been approaching but which she now seemed to be leaving behind.

Nessie and the Boggart, surfacing, watched her with satisfaction, and swam cheerfully away.

The Boggart turned into a seal, and made a figure-eight dive.

"Don't do that!" said Nessie plaintively, as he surfaced again. *"You make me feel so stupid."*

The Boggart turned back into a boggart. He said with longing, "*We could have such fun, if you'd only learn how again. We could go all the way to Loch Linnhe and Castle Keep—my castle wasn't blown up. We could live there and tease my family, and play with the seals.*"

"*I cannae stay boggart-shape long enough,*" Nessie said.

"*You could swim all the way there, now. They made a canal to join the lochs a hundred years ago—you can swim from Loch Ness to the western sea!*"

But this news not only failed to fill Nessie with delight, it enveloped him in such fear that the water all around him chilled almost to freezing. He looked at the Boggart in terror, and he changed instantly back into monster form and sank down, down toward the mud.

The Boggart groaned, and dived after him.

* * *

AS THEY PILED out of Mr. Maconochie's car, Harold Pindle waved merrily at them, and made extravagant beckoning gestures. He still wore his battered sweatshirt and faded jeans, but Emily thought he had probably changed his shirt; the collar jutting out of the sweatshirt looked cleaner than before. And his long grey hair showed signs of having been combed.

He beamed at them as they crossed the parking lot. "Allow me to present Axel Kalling, our wonderful sponsor," he said. "Axel, these are my co-witnesses—Emily,

Jessup, Tommy, and Mr. Maconochie of Castle Keep."

The small, neat man at Harold's side gave them a small, neat bow, so formally that he almost seemed to click his heels. He wore an old-fashioned dark grey suit with wide flat lapels, and his thick white hair was cut to a carefully elegant shape. Two strongly-marked clefts ran down past his mouth, but the eyes above them were bright and alert, and fanned with little laughter-lines.

"Emily is the name of my sister," he said, crinkling the laughter-lines at Emily. "She grows sweet peas, they smell most delicious, but her llamas eat them if she is not careful."

Emily blinked at him. "Her llamas? "she said.

"I look forward so great to the Worm!" said Mr. Kalling warmly. He had a surprisingly deep voice, with the lilting Swedish accent that takes the end of every sentence up and then down. "And tomorrow night the moon is full! Is that not right, Mr. Maconnie?"

"Er," said Mr. Maconochie, taken by surprise. "Uh. Yes, I expect so, yes." He looked down at Mr. Kalling in wonder and bafflement.

"Worm will like that," Mr. Kalling said, nodding his head firmly.

"This way, folks. This way to the great Monster show, in the screening room! Axel's flown in to see the tape from yesterday." Harold was shepherding them across the parking lot, toward a trailer less boxlike than the first. It had windows, and a bright red door, which he flung open.

"Good!" said Mr. Kalling. He trotted briskly inside,

and Harold paused just long enough to flash a quick grin over his shoulder.

"Not crazy, not really," he whispered. "He's a great guy, just—different." He disappeared after Mr. Kalling.

"And *very* rich," said Mr. Maconochie. He took a matchbox out of his pocket and held it up, and under the familiar label that they had never really examined before they saw the words: KALLING MATCH.

Chuck the technician was crunching toward them across the parking lot, with a backpack over his shoulder. He no longer wore his MEAN MAN T-shirt, but his expression was no more cordial than before. "You on your way in, or out?" he said, unsmiling.

Emily flashed him a beautiful smile. "We're following you in."

Chuck grunted unappreciatively, and marched past her.

Inside, the second trailer was quite different from the first. After a small office, with desks and telephones and a fax machine, they found themselves in a thick-carpeted space filled with comfortable armchairs and an enormous television set. Chuck opened his backpack and began fitting what looked like a miniature video-tape into a machine beside the television. He crouched beside it, twiddling dials. From one of the chairs Harold waved an expansive welcoming arm. Then he bounced to his feet, as they all settled themselves around the largest armchair, which Mr. Kalling was occupying as if it were a throne.

"Axel Kalling, my friend," Harold said, in clear careful tones as if he were making a speech, "before we see this amazing tape, I want you to know how utterly delighted I am that your trust in this project has been rewarded."

Mr. Kalling nodded his white head impatiently. "Happy for sight of the Worm," he said.

But Harold wasn't to be rushed. He hadn't finished. He *was* making a speech.

"Without your faith and your financing, none of our research would have been possible," he said solemnly, each word weighing at least fifteen pounds. "No other man on this planet could have had the foresight and the imagination to set up the Kalling-Pindle operation. I want you to know that what you are about to see now— the shattering images that we all witnessed yesterday— these are the justification and reward for your generosity. And they will engrave your name in the annals of scientific history." He paused, looking misty-eyed at Mr. Kalling, and then suddenly his face split into a great joyous grin and, to everyone's great relief, he was his bouncy enthusiastic self again. "Hit it, Chuck!" he said.

The lights went out, and the television screen grew bright, and turned green. Chuck sat back from his dials, to watch.

Something made Emily put her right hand into her pocket. She found the little cockle shell there, pressing into her fingers, and for an instant had an odd impression that it had summoned her. She clutched it instinctively as she gazed at the screen.

"This is the laser image," Harold whispered. "Gradually you'll see the creature coming toward us, getting closer, becoming clearer. And then we switch to video from the surface—and my God, Axel, it's such a sight!"

They all stared at the green rectangle. It glowed at them, and flickered a little. But nothing appeared on it at all.

They waited. And waited. The screen remained blank.

Harold said impatiently, "What's wrong, Chuck?"

Chuck peered at his dials. He pressed a button, he turned a knob. The green square flickered, but remained empty.

"For Pete's sake," said Harold. "We watched it over and over, last night, and it was fine. Is this the right tape?"

"Yes," said Chuck. He swallowed hard. Emily began to feel sorry for him. His fingers moved desperately to and fro, and he switched the television off, then on again. The picture vanished and then grew, still green, still empty.

"Oh dear!" Emily said. "There's still nothing there!"

"We can see that!" said Chuck nastily, and her sympathy for him dwindled. Minutes went by as they stared at the blank screen. Irritably Harold pushed Chuck aside and played with the controls himself, but nothing changed. Finally there was a click, and the screen changed from green to black.

"This is impossible!" Frenziedly Harold rewound the tape and began trying again, to be faced once more with the same unchanging flat green image. He groaned, and clutched his thinning grey hair.

Emily realized suddenly that her fingers were hurting from the pressure of the cockle shell. She let it go, and took her hand out of her pocket.

Axel Kalling said gravely, "But you took pictures of Worm, did you not, Harold?"

"It was there on the screen, I swear it was!" said Harold Pindle, distraught. He looked wildly around him. "Wasn't it, kids?"

His distress was so acute that none of them could bear to try to explain to him about the erratic behavior of boggarts. "We did see it, all of us, Mr. Kalling!" said Jessup bravely. "A real plesiosaur, humongous, all dripping—and Jenny was out there and she smelled it, it smelled of fish!"

"It was just like the pictures of Nessie," Tommy said.

"It really was!" Emily said.

Axel Kalling turned his well-cut white head to Mr. Maconochie. "Well, Mr. Maconnie? Did you too see this Worm?"

Mr. Maconochie stood up, tall and silent under the low ceiling of the trailer, and Jessup, Emily and Tommy looked at him with sudden misgiving. But he nodded his head slowly.

"Yes," he said. "We saw it clear enough on the screens, the big body and the long neck and the wee head. Just for a few moments, mind, and only on the screens. But it was good and clear."

There was a pause, and then Axel Kalling let out a sudden shrill cackle of laughter. They all stared at him. His bright eyes glittered at them from the neat little figure sitting doll-like in the tall chair.

"This is shy Worm!" he said merrily. "He does not want picture to be taken! He remove himself from your machine!"

Harold snapped the tape out of its slot, with an angry click. "It's a technical failure, Axel, and I apologize more than I can tell you. We'll see if there's some way of fixing it." He thrust the tape at Chuck, with a cold glare, and Chuck pushed his way sullenly out of the trailer.

But Axel was still cackling. "No no, is quite fine, do not worry, Harold! I am *happy* with shy Worm, I was shy too in my youth days!" He stood up, patting Harold on the arm and beaming around the small room. "I shall go happy back to Stockholm now, and you will creep up on Worm one day when he is not looking, and take picture then. And he cannot then take himself off your screen if he does not know that he is there. Yes?"

Harold moaned softly. "Oh Axel, please—this is a solid prehistoric survivor, not a creature from outer space. Wait for Chuck to fix the tape—I want you to see the evidence."

But Axel Kalling was on his feet. "No problems, Harold! You are doing wonderful, I am very pleased." He marched briskly over the carpeted floor of the trailer to the doorway, calling in musical Swedish to the driver of the long black car that stood waiting in the parking lot. As the car door opened, he glanced back over his shoulder and beamed at them.

"Good-bye, little Emily!" he called. "Watch for Worm, and my sister will send you llama!"

He disappeared inside the car, and it slid away.

"He probably means that," Harold said. He rubbed his head ruefully. "Oh Lord, what a disaster. I guess we were just in too much of a hurry to get those pictures on tape. Chuck must have blown it somehow. Wiped them off by accident. I can't *believe* this happened!"

Emily said diffidently, "D'you think maybe . . . Mr. Kalling might be right, about it not wanting to be photographed?"

Harold Pindle looked at her indulgently, and laughed. He straightened his back, and his face began to brighten with new determination. "Come on, Emily honey, get real—we've *seen* this beast now, we know it exists. It's in that loch, and there's no way it can escape the Kalling-Pindle survey. Soon as I possibly can I'm going to put Sydney and Adelaide down there to comb every inch of Loch Ness—every square inch of the bottom, with sonar boats checking all the water above it. We're on our way!"

He beamed around at them all, as they looked at him with assorted degrees of misgiving and dismay.

"Stick around, kids! You're in on the last great search, the one that'll really find the Monster. We're going to make history!"

SEVEN

✳

A<small>NGUS</small> C<small>AMERON</small> swallowed the last bite
of his cheese-and-tomato sandwich. He was sitting in
the railway station cafe in the town of Fort William,
having called in at the station to pick up a new
timetable. When he was not away chasing a story he
drove to Fort William once a week, in his elderly but
reliable little van, to pick up any extra supplies his wife
needed for the Port Appin store.

He stood up, and took his empty plate to the
counter. "Cup of tea, please, Marge."

"With milk and two sugar," said Marge, "and a
chocolate biscuit for afters." She was a large, billowy,
smiling lady with a high pile of blonde hair, and a soft
spot for regular customers.

"Aye," said Angus. "And a nice juicy murder,
please. Or even a scandal in City Hall. *Anything*, for a bit
of news in this town."

Marge poured him his tea. She said cheerfully,
"I'll hit my husband over the head with a bottle

when I go home tonight. You'll be the first to know."

Angus grinned, and took his cup.

Beside him, a precise, accented voice said clearly, "A cup of your delicious coffee, please. Black."

Angus turned, to see who could be lunatic enough to describe British railway coffee as delicious, and saw the immaculate white head of Axel Kalling. "Mr. Kalling!" he said. "I thought you'd gone back to Sweden."

Axel Kalling blinked up at him. He smiled, courteous but vague.

"Angus Cameron," said Angus helpfully, holding out his hand. "I interviewed you for the Glasgow Herald."

"Of course!" said Mr. Kalling, and shook the hand heartily. "Ah well yes, I went home, but here I am again. We flew in yesterday, my assistant Nils and I. But really I do not like to fly, so now we take train to Newcastle and ferry to Goteborg. The sea, the wonderful sea, Mr. Cameron!"

"Black coffee," said Marge, cautiously handing him a cup.

"Allow me," said Angus. He put down some money and took both tea and coffee to his table. Axel Kalling followed him, with the ease of a man accustomed to being looked after, and sat down. "Most kind," he said. "I shall wait for Nils—he gets tickets." Then he leaned forward to Angus conspiratorially, with a glint in his bright old eyes.

"We have found Worm!" he whispered.

"What?" Angus said.

"Worm! He has found him, my friend Professor Pindle! He has found your Loch Ness Monster!"

Angus eyed him carefully, and stirred his tea. It had taken him only the first two minutes of his interview with Axel Kalling to classify him as a charming but hopeless nut case. In his career as a journalist he had met several lunatics, and at least half of them had claimed to have seen the Loch Ness Monster. He said cautiously, "Did you see him?"

"Of course! He is very happy, he calls me instantly on telephone!"

"No, Mr. Kalling, not Professor Pindle—the Monster."

Axel Kalling gave his high-pitched cackle of laughter. "Ah—*he* has not called me yet. But soon perhaps!" He sipped his coffee, and looked mischievously at Angus over the top of the cup. "No, I did not see Worm. But Professor Pindle saw him very clear, with his laser instruments. The great Worm, with the long neck. Just as we were hoping for, Mr. Cameron!"

"So the professor showed you pictures?" Angus said.

"Pictures did not come out," said Mr. Kalling.

Angus tried valiantly not to smile. "No. It's a funny thing—they never do."

Axel Kalling wagged a finger at him. "You journalists! You have no faith! Worm appeared to many people, not just to my Harold. To his assistants, two of them. To a lawyer. And to some children. All these people swore solemnly they saw Worm!"

"Children?" said Angus skeptically.

Axel Kalling nodded his white head vigorously. "One of these children is named after my sister!"

"Indeed," Angus said. He took a gloomy swig of tea, and longed again for news of a murder. Perhaps he could write a story about unbalanced foreign monster-hunters? No, no, it had been done too often before. . . .

A straight-backed young man in a dark suit came and stood respectfully in front of Axel Kalling and addressed him in Swedish. Mr. Kalling got up, and wagged his finger again at Angus. "We go," he said. *"Tak for coffee.* But I am shocked you do not believe word of lawyer. Especially when he is good Scottish lawyer."

He grinned at Angus, and followed the young man toward the station door. As Angus watched him go, he found a few of the lilting accented words echoing through his head, persistent, nudging . . . *some children . . . good Scottish lawyer.* . . . He jumped to his feet, calling out, as the Swedes reached the door.

"Mr. Kalling! How many children were there?"

Axel Kalling looked back over his shoulder. He said, "Three."

Angus blinked. "And—what's your sister's name?"

"Emily," said Axel Kalling. He waved, and disappeared.

* * *

ANGUS SAID into the telephone, "But suppose, just suppose the reports were genuine. Really true."

"Who's to say what's true?" said the weary voice of the News Editor from the newsroom of the *Glasgow Herald*. "Come on, Angus. We've both been through this before. *Anyone* can claim to have seen Nessie swimming along—when there just didn't happen to be a camera handy by."

"I know," Angus said gloomily.

"Just three days ago we had a respectable medical doctor in here claiming he'd been riding in a UFO with little green men."

"I know," Angus said again. "Old Doc Grant. He tries it every summer."

"I want proof," said the News Editor. "No proof, no story."

"All right, George."

"Listen, you want to go there, go. There's not much else happening, Lord knows. But even if you see the Monster with your very own eyes it's no story unless I get pictures. Great big beautiful clear pictures. Savvy?"

"Okay," said Angus Cameron.

"*Pictures!*" said the News Editor.

* * *

NESSIE LAY SULKING, a mountainous heap on the muddy bottom of the loch. "*I belong here. I don't want to leave. Don't keep on at me.*"

"*But you're a boggart, you should be having fun,*" the Boggart said urgently. "*With me. Out under the sun and the stars, out in the air and the sea. Out there enjoying life, not lying here like a blob!"* He turned an agitated somersault, in a whirl of cold sparks of light. *"Don't you remember it all? Wasn't it fun turning round the girl in her boat the other day? Don't you remember the old days, playing with the seals?"*

"I do. And it was," Nessie said, begrudgingly but with a glimmer of boggart mischief. Then he drooped again. *"But I've lived here too long, cuz. I haven't the heart to leave. This is my home."* He stretched out his huge neck and laid his head on the mud.

The Boggart flittered to and fro above him, a restless glimmer in the cool dark water. He was not used to anxiety, to the distress of affection. Unhappiness flowed all around him, like a murky cloud. He longed to bring his forlorn cousin back to the proper life of a boggart, and he had no idea of what to do. Unheard in the deep loch, he whimpered plaintively.

* * *

"LISTEN!" EMILY SAID. She peered out over the tangled hawthorn hedge, toward the distant glint of Loch Ness. They had driven back to the campground to pick up Mr. Maconochie's favorite pipe, which he had left in his tent. He carried two or three other pipes in his car, together with a plentiful supply of tobacco, but this particular pipe was a kind of comforting talisman. They saw it clenched firmly between his teeth now as he emerged from his tent, zipping the door closed behind him.

Jessup shook his head in wonder. "I suppose the best you can say is that he doesn't actually smoke it much."

"It's his security blanket," Tommy said wisely. He slid out of the driving seat of Mr. Maconochie's car, where he had been practicing imaginary gearshifts.

"*Listen!*" Emily said again insistently, from the hedge.

"What is it?" said Mr. Maconochie through his teeth and his pipe, as he came back to them.

"Didn't you hear it? A kind of wail. A sad noise."

"Where?"

"I don't know. In the air, sort of."

"It's a bird," said Jessup. "The greater speckled wailer, native to the west coast of Scotland."

"It wasn't a bird."

Tommy looked at her more closely, and came over and patted her briefly on the shoulder. "You all right, Em?"

"I guess so. It was just such a sad noise." Emily gave her head a shake, and turned back to them. "What are we going to do about Harold?"

"I don't think there's anything to be done," Mr. Maconochie said. "He'll send Sydney and Adelaide out to do an elaborate survey of the loch, and perhaps they'll pick up the Monster. But if the Monster is indeed a boggart, it'll disappear, just as it did when we were watching."

"Harold got pictures, though," Emily said.

"And they disappeared too," said Tommy.

"That could just have been a technical hitch, like he said."

"There's something more complicated going on," Jessup said. He chewed his thumbnail. "Why did our Boggart give me that dream? I know it was him. And where *is* our Boggart?"

Tommy said to the air, "Boggart? Are you there? *Bheil thu an sin?*"

They looked around, at the windblown trees, at the cloud-patched blue sky, but found no kind of answer anywhere.

"I don't know what that wailing sound was, but it was really unhappy," Emily said.

"I think he wants us to go to Castle Urquhart," Jessup said. "It was Nessie's place and he wants us to go there. But I don't know why."

Mr. Maconochie took his pipe out of his mouth and stuffed it into his jacket pocket. He opened the car door.

"Come on, then," he said. "I'll buy us a picnic lunch on the way."

* * *

WHIRLING IN A TINY invisible eddy, the Boggart hovered persistently over Nessie's recumbent head.

"*Castle Urquhart!*" he whispered. "*Castle Urquhart!*"

"*Leave me alone,*" Nessie said. He nuzzled his head down into the soft mud.

"*I havenae seen your castle for centuries. Take me there.*"

"*My castle's ruined. They blew it up.*"

"It's not gone. It's still there, ruined or not. Come on, cuz, just this once, just for me. Take me there."

Nessie made muffled, snuffling noises of protest into the dark mud that was his bed, and then, with great reluctance, raised his long neck. "All right. Because it's you asking. But I'm no treat to be with, these days—I'm not good at fun any more. You'd be happier if you left me on my own."

"Castle Urquhart!" said the Boggart, darting to and fro, visible now as a little whirling flurry of phosphorescence in the black water. "Come on!"

Busy as a pilot fish he swam off down the loch, and Nessie lifted his huge bulk from the bottom of the loch and came after him, driving himself through the water with great sweeps of his powerful flippers. They headed south, toward Castle Urquhart.

And above them, on the Inverness road, Harold Pindle, Chuck, Jenny and several local Scottish assistants drove in the opposite direction toward the northern end of the loch, in a small convoy. They were headed for the point from which Sydney and Adelaide and half a dozen survey boats, all their electronic searching equipment humming with life, would be launched into the water to examine the entire loch. Inexorably south they would go, submerged, unstopping, from one end of the loch to the other, scouring every inch of the water in a search that no large creature could possibly escape.

*　*　*

WHEN THE RANGE ROVER turned into the parking lot of

the little cafe along the road back to Castle Urquhart, it was Tommy and Jessup who were detailed to go in and buy sandwiches. Mr. Maconochie had caught sight of a nursery on the opposite side of the road, with a discreet noticeboard reading FLOWERS, SHRUBS, HEATHS AND HEATHERS. His eyes lit up.

"Look!" he said. "Just what I need!"

Emily had a quick mental image of the windswept rocky islet on which Castle Keep stood. "But you haven't got a garden," she said.

"There are little pockets of soil here and there," said Mr. Maconochie defensively. "Heather is very hardy, heather would be just the thing. I shall go and enquire."

"I'll come too," Emily said.

"Lunch!" said Jessup plaintively.

Mr. Maconochie pulled some bills from his wallet and thrust them at him. "You and Tommy can go buy us a picnic—we shan't be long."

The boys scrambled out of the car, and Mr. Maconochie performed some elaborate turning maneuvers and roared across the road and up the nursery's curving unpaved driveway. When he turned off the engine, silence swallowed them so completely that Emily found herself trying to open and shut the car door without making a sound. Suddenly they were in a very peaceful place: a haven of green and growing things, without a human being to be seen anywhere. Racks of plants and flowers stretched all around, and beyond them a small wood of shrubs and trees, some growing in pots, some anchored to the ground by roots that had grown out of ancient, long-undisturbed sacking. Somewhere a solitary bird was singing, a long sweet chirruping trill. Looking around, Emily felt that she was in somebody's garden, a private refuge; that if this were a shop, it was the shop of someone who could never bear anything to be sold.

Neither she nor Mr. Maconochie spoke. They drifted among the rows of plants, separate yet together, in a daze of peacefulness. Emily thought of her father, on the rare days when he had time to work in their little city garden in Toronto; he would seem to spend hours, sometimes, on one small job like pruning a rosebush. Slowly and dreamily he would take hold of a stem and stare at its buds and leaves, waiting until he seemed to have learned its whole length by heart before he carefully raised the clippers and made one small gentle cut. It was as though time moved at a different speed, for gardeners.

She gazed at an array of small pots of heathers, and tried to choose one of them to take back to Toronto to remind Robert Volnik of Scotland. Their tiny leaves ranged through every shade of green from dark olive to almost-yellow, and of those that were in flower, the blossoms were pink or purple or any of twenty colors in between. Mr. Maconochie, moving very slowly and carefully, was picking out a pot here, a pot there, and setting them in a little line on the ground. Like Emily, he seemed to be in a happy trance.

A quiet voice said, "Can I help you, my dear?"

Emily jumped, and looked around. Very close, she saw an old lady smiling at her: a warm, welcoming smile in a soft-skinned face creased by hundreds of fine lines.

She was a small old lady, shorter than Emily, with white hair as snowy as Mr. Kalling's but far more wild and wispy. She wore jeans, a blue corduroy shirt and bright red Wellington boots.

Emily said impulsively, "I love your boots."

The old lady laughed. "And my heathers?" she said.

"Oh of course. I want one I can take to Toronto for my dad's garden. It gets pretty cold there."

"It gets pretty cold here too," the old lady said equably. "But I'm not sure Canadian Customs will let you take one to Toronto. They worry about importing evil foreign insects."

"Oh!" said Emily in disappointment.

"Maybe if you washed all the soil off the roots," said the old lady. "And wrapped it in a wet paper towel."

"We'll look up the rules, Emily," said Mr. Maconochie, appearing at her side with an armful of small pots. "Choose yourself a heather and I'll buy it for you."

"This one," said Emily promptly, picking up a plant covered in tiny, sturdy purple flowers. "Thank you, Mr. Mac."

"*Erica vulgaris*. Very hardy," said the old lady approvingly. "An excellent choice." Her eye traveled over the pots in Mr. Maconochie's arms. "And so are these. My goodness, you have quite remarkable taste, you people. Come along into my office."

She led them toward a long, low greenhouse tucked behind the rows of plants. It was filled with long tables bearing rows of very small heathers in very small pots, and it bore no resemblance to an office except that in one corner there was a battered wooden desk and two canvas chairs, one on either side of it. On the desk were a cash register, a cup of tea and a sleeping cat.

Mr. Maconochie followed her meekly, clutching his pots. He had to duck his head to go through the door. "It's a very exposed area, where I live," he said. "And the soil's pretty poor. I hope they won't mind."

"For the right person, my dear, they will grow anywhere," the old lady said. "Where *do* you live?" She pulled off one of her red Wellington boots and tipped out a small stone, without holding onto anything for balance. Mr. Maconochie watched in admiration.

"Port Appin," he said. "Castle Keep."

In the middle of pulling her boot back on, the old lady suddenly lost her balance completely. She clutched at her desk, and recovered herself.

"Castle Keep," she said. "Well, well. Are you the new owner?"

"That's right," said Mr. Maconochie. "Emily here inherited it, or rather her father did, and I bought it from him."

"Really," said the old lady. She took Mr. Maconochie's heathers from him one by one and began packing them into a low-sided cardboard box. "And is it a quiet life you have there?"

Emily glanced at her sharply. It seemed an odd question, from a stranger. But the lined old face was smiling and open.

Mr. Maconochie said guardedly, "Most of the time."

"Devon MacDevon was a good friend of mine," the old lady said. "Many years ago, when I was young." She took a miniature pair of clippers, and carefully trimmed off a broken shoot from one of the heathers.

"Did you know his sister?" Emily said.

The old lady laughed. "The black lamb of the family? No, my dear, I am very old but not quite as old as that. But I remember the story. She ran away with a Campbell, and married him, so the family never spoke to her again."

"We are a foolish, tribal race," Mr. Maconochie said, lighting his pipe. "With long memories."

"We are that. She and her husband went abroad, I believe."

"To Canada. She was my great-grandmother," Emily said proudly.

"Was she now?" said the old lady, smiling at her, and for an instant Emily had the strong, startling impression that this piece of news was not news to her at all. "Then you are a MacDevon, and the first one to have stood amongst my heathers for a very long time." She fed some numbers into the cash register, and looked up at Mr. Maconochie.

"Eight at three-fifty, that will be twenty-eight pounds," she said.

"Very reasonable," said Mr. Maconochie, and he wrote her a check, being a careful and reactionary man who did not approve of credit cards.

The old lady studied the check. "James U. Maconochie," she read. She looked up at him again, and

Emily saw that she had very green eyes, like his own. "So you would be an Urquhart, Mr. Maconochie."

She punched at the cash register, which made a resounding *ping* and woke up the sleeping cat. The cat stretched, purring. It was completely black, from its nose to its tail.

"My mother was an Urquhart," Mr. Maconochie said.

"I didn't know that," said Emily. She looked with interest at the old lady, whom she was beginning to suspect of being a friendly witch. "How did *you* know that?"

"Not many names begin with the letter U in this country," said the old lady mildly. "And besides, I am Miss Mary Urquhart. How do you do?"

She held out a small strong hand, and first Emily and then Mr. Maconochie shook it, politely. "How do you do?" they said in turn.

There was an eruption of noise through the open door of the greenhouse, and the black cat jumped down to the ground. Tommy and Jessup came in, their arms full of paper bags. "We bought a lot!" Jessup said with satisfaction. "Sodas too. And if you want it, there's a touristy talk at the castle in ten minutes' time."

"This is Miss Urquhart," Emily said. "Miss Mary Urquhart."

Suddenly still, the boys stared at the old lady. She smiled at them, untroubled.

"Wow!" Jessup said. "Do you own Urquhart Castle?"

"It belongs these days to the National Trust for Scotland," Miss Urquhart said. "But you could say that by blood I am still part of it, and so is your Mr. Maconochie, from his mother's side. Just as you and your sister are still part of Castle Keep."

Jessup's eyes went from Miss Urquhart's face to Emily's and back again, curious. They were saying to Emily: *Who is this person, and how does she know about us?*

"So Mr. Maconochie is one of the links between both castles, now that he has bought your own," Miss Urquhart added.

Tommy said, *"One* of the links?" There was a challenge in his voice, and like Jessup, he was watching her cautiously. The two of them reminded Emily of young dogs meeting a stranger; sniffing warily, unsure whether to wag their tails or bark.

"Miss Urquhart is a link herself," said Mr. Maconochie. "She used to know old Mr. MacDevon."

The old lady smiled at Tommy, and closed Mr. Maconochie's check inside her cash register with a smart *ping.* "You must be Tommy Cameron," she said. "He was very fond of you."

Tommy flushed a little, looking pleased, and she rose briskly to her feet. Reaching for a cardboard sign reading OPEN, which was hanging inside the greenhouse's front windowpane, she turned it around to read CLOSED. "Now that I've made this excellent sale," she said, "I think I shall shut up shop for the day. And if you would care for it, I will cross the street with you and tell you a few things about the castle far more interesting than those that the tourists would hear."

"Great!" said Jessup.

"That would be very kind," Mr. Maconochie said, picking up his box of heather pots. "And I hope you will share our picnic lunch."

"What will you tell us about?" said Emily, as they filed out of the greenhouse.

Miss Urquhart turned a large rusty key in the lock, and put it in her jeans pocket. "Well, for one thing, of course," she said, "boggarts."

EIGHT

✳

THEY SAT ON THE GRASS with their backs to one of the ruined walls of Castle Urquhart, eating ham sandwiches. The castle's other visitors had all drifted away to examine the tower, the only part of the castle that remained at least partly intact.

"I remember when I was a girl hearing a vague old tale that a boggart used to live in this castle before it was blown up," Miss Urquhart said. "A family trickster, an invisible creature. But that was so long ago that I never gave the story much thought—I mean, the castle's been a ruin for more than three hundred years. It was only when I went to stay with Devon MacDevon that I learned about boggarts properly."

She took a long thoughtful drag at the straw sticking out of her can of Pepsi-Cola, which looked almost as incongruous next to her snow-white hair as the red Wellington boots.

"You met *our* Boggart," said Jessup with pride.

"Not exactly. Your Boggart tried to get rid of me.

Salt in my drinking water, sand in my soap dish, thistles in my bed. All his tricks said loud and clear, *go home*. My brother was staying at Castle Keep too, but nothing at all happened to him."

"Oh dear," Emily said. "Why didn't the Boggart like you?"

"To tell the truth," said Miss Urquhart, "I think he was afraid I was wanting to marry the MacDevon."

"And were you?" Jessup said.

"Jess!" said Emily.

"Oh, that's all right," Miss Urquhart said. She smiled, rather wistfully, and Emily could suddenly see the echo of a pretty young face inside the old, lined one. "I did find him very attractive, I must say. But I was only in my early twenties, and he was forty-five at least, and already set in his ways. He never did marry anyone. I think perhaps he found it easier to live with a boggart than with a wife."

"That was his loss," said Mr. Maconochie gallantly, even though he had never wanted to live with a wife either.

"Have a chocolate biscuit," Tommy said.

"Thank you," said Miss Urquhart to both of them, and she took a biscuit. "Anyway, he spoke to me quite openly about the Boggart, and apologized for him. And when I came home I found myself coming quite often to this castle, here where we sit now, and listening for our own boggart."

Mr. Maconochie said, "Listening?"

"That's the only word I can think of for it," Miss Urquhart said. She took a bite of her chocolate biscuit.

"Feeling what he's feeling," said Emily. She thought of the sad wail she had heard from the loch that morning, which nobody else had been able to hear.

"That's right," said Miss Urquhart.

"Hmm," said Mr. Maconochie noncommittally.

Miss Urquhart ate the rest of her biscuit, got to her feet and held out a hand to him. "Come with me and I'll show you," she said.

"What?" said Mr. Maconochie. He peered up at her through his bristly grey eyebrows.

"Come!" Miss Urquhart stood there small and insistent, holding out her hand. "You are an Urquhart and so am I, and with that much family feeling focused on Nessie, we shall hear what he is feeling. You just have to concentrate. I'll show you."

Since she showed no sign of moving, Mr. Maconochie, looking very skeptical, unfolded his long legs and stood up, and the old lady took his hand and led him toward the outer wall of the castle. Beyond it, a little path ran along the top of a grassy slope overlooking the loch. Like a mother settling a small child, she sat him down on the edge of the path, looking out over the water, and sat herself beside him. Loch Ness lay below them, and from its further bank the forested green hillside rose to ridges of bare rock.

Emily, Jessup and Tommy stayed behind, in the grass-wrapped center of the castle.

"Okay then, Jess," said Emily. "The Boggart wanted us to come here, you said—and we've come. So what happens next?"

"Beats me," Jessup said.

"Maybe it's already happening," said Tommy. "Maybe it's Miss Urquhart, and the listening."

* * *

NESSIE SLOWED DOWN, and drifted upward a little, closer to the surface of the water. The Boggart could see it like a glimmering ceiling several feet above them.

"*My castle's just over that way,*" Nessie said. "*My poor ruined castle.*"

"*Take boggart-shape,*" the Boggart said, "*and we'll go up and have a look.*"

Nessie groaned. "*I'm tired, cuz. You've no idea how exhausting it is, hauling all this weight around. I need a rest.*"

"*If you'd just practice your shape-shifting,*" said the Boggart in exasperation, "*you'd have no weight at all.*"

"*A wee nap,*" Nessie said. "*A wee nap, that's what I need.*" And he closed his eyes and slowly sank, yet again, huge and inert, to the bottom of the loch.

The Boggart twirled irritably and invisibly in the water, giving a considerable fright to two small lake trout who suddenly found themselves revolving upside down, and he shot up to the surface and out into the air. Just for the pleasure of flying with wings, he shifted his shape to that of a golden eagle, the rarest and most powerful bird in all Scotland. He soared up out of the water, and a bird-watching clergyman from Dundee, peering through his binoculars from his folding canvas chair on the bank, was so surprised and delighted that he nearly fell into the loch. He went home and wrote an ecstatic letter to the *Times*, and for years afterward his sermons glowed with an image of hope and wonder: the great golden eagle that he had seen so improbably fly up out of the dark waters of Loch Ness.

The Boggart wheeled over the loch, high up, resting on his wings. Far at the northern end of the long lake he could see something strange: a line of boats, spread across the whole width of the loch, moving in unison, very slowly, toward him.

* * *

ANGUS CAMERON WAS writing busily in his notebook, in the control room of the Kalling-Pindle Project's trailer. Squashed between the back of Harold Pindle's chair and a very knobbly bank of batteries, he barely had space to turn a page.

"So what speed are they moving at?" he asked.

"Two knots," Harold said. "Very slow. Very thorough. But they have a good burst of speed if they should need to chase anything."

"And nothing can get past them?"

"Nothing of any real size. The ROVs are scanning the deep water while the sonar on the boats takes care of the top two hundred feet. They are covering every inch of this loch, and the screens will show anything they meet that's larger than a two-pound salmon. Today or tomorrow, Mr. Cameron! This is it!"

He pulled his earphones over his ears and sat peering happily at his array of blank green screens, with Chuck beside him intent on gauges and dials. The air in the little room prickled with tension.

Behind them, Angus Cameron was overcome by a great wave of disbelief. He had seen all this too often before: the passionate monster-hunters, bubbling with hope and conviction, longing to be the first to prove that Nessie was really there. They always knew they were going to find proof, and they never found it. Over the years, only the technology changed.

He shut his notebook. In spite of all those boats and screens and submersibles, he knew that he was being driven to chase this story not by any faith in the Kalling-Pindle expedition, but by the hint of possibility that his own son, his levelheaded skeptical Tommy, might actually have seen the Loch Ness Monster. If Tommy were to swear to its existence, even without pictures, then Angus would become the most passionate monster-hunter of all.

"Thanks, Dr. Pindle," he said. "I'll be back later, if I may."

"Feel free," said Harold, his eyes on the screens. "Sorry I don't know where the kids have gone. Try the campground."

"I'll find them," Angus said.

* * *

EMILY SHIVERED, and opened her eyes. She had been lying on her back on the grass, listening to a lark's faint bubbling song, while the boys went off to investigate the tower, but now a large billowing cloud was crossing the sun, and the air was suddenly cool. She sat up, reaching for her sweater, and saw Tommy and Jessup scrambling back toward her over the ruined walls. High above her the lark was still singing. Emily looked up, but could see no sign of it; only a speck that was a much larger bird, some kind of hawk perhaps, drifting to and fro very high in the sky.

Jessup came skidding down beside her as she pulled the sweater over her head. "Here they come," he said. "Over there!"

Tommy said, "Mr. Mac looks a bit green."

Miss Urquhart came toward them from the castle's outer wall, a small neat figure in her jeans and red boots, with Mr. Maconochie behind her. He folded his long legs and sat down next to Emily on a pile of rock, and took out his pipe and tobacco pouch. "Oh my," he said.

Emily studied his face. "Are you all right?" she said.

Miss Urquhart helped herself to a chocolate biscuit, and passed the box to Tommy. "He's all right," she said. "But poor Nessie is not happy at all."

"That was very strange indeed," Mr. Maconochie said slowly. He peered absently into the bowl of his pipe, as if it might explain something to him. "We sat there . . . listening, I suppose. And then it was like . . . being inside somebody else's emotions. Feeling them as if they were yours, even though they weren't. It's very hard to describe."

"Yes, it is," said Emily comfortingly.

Jessup said, "So what does Nessie feel?"

"Frightened," said Mr. Maconochie.

"And restless," Miss Urquhart said. "He wants to change but he's forgotten how."

Mr. Maconochie waved his pipe stem at them like a pointer. "And he wants to stay but he wants to leave. Wants to be with our Boggart but wants to be left alone." He paused. "Most of all it was like hearing someone calling, 'Help, help!'"

"So was the dream the Boggart gave me," Jessup said. "Showing the two of them together, wanting things to be like that again."

Tommy squatted beside him and passed him the box of biscuits. He said, "The only thing missing is that they don't tell you *how* to help."

"But they can't do that because they aren't actually talking, you're just plugged into them," Jessup said, intent, trying to remember. "It's like—oh I don't know, it's hard to understand without having it happen to you."

Tommy stood up again. He said rather stiffly, "Well, I am neither a MacDevon nor an Urquhart, so I dare say I am not qualified to understand."

"That's not what I meant," Jessup said.

Tommy said, "Though we are all more Scottish than you will ever be, boggarts and all."

"Tommy!" Jessup said plaintively.

Emily got to her feet hastily, found herself standing closer to Tommy's stiff hostile form than she had intended, but plowed ahead nonetheless. "I think this is all just about both boggarts wanting to be together," she said. "And not knowing how, because there's all this space in the way. And that's tough."

She looked valiantly into Tommy's coldly glinting blue eyes, and he looked back at her. He said quietly, "I know about space getting in the way, for friends."

"I mean," said Emily, growing rather pink, "I mean, maybe there's something we can do to help them be together, if we can just find out what it is."

"Hey!" said a cheerful voice above them, from the path to the tower. "I finally tracked you down!"

They looked up, startled, and saw the smiling face of Angus Cameron.

Taken by surprise, Tommy stared up at his father with a marked lack of welcome. "What are you doing here?" he demanded.

Angus scrambled down over the rocky ledge to stand beside them. His neck was festooned with leather straps, and camera bags and binocular cases hung from them, bumping against his hips.

"It's amazing how many Range Rovers full of camping gear there are in the parking lots of Argyll," he said. "But only Mr. Mac's has Emily's 'Save the Whales' sticker on its back window." He suddenly noticed Miss Urquhart next to him, and stuck out his hand to her. "Excuse me," he said politely. "I'm Angus Cameron."

"Mary Urquhart," said Miss Urquhart amiably.

"He's my dad," Tommy said.

"Is anything wrong, Angus?" said Mr. Maconochie.

"No no, not at all. I was just passing by."

"You were not passing by, you said you were tracking us down," said Tommy warily. "I'm a big boy now, Dad, you don't have to check up on me."

"Did you bring William?" said Emily hopefully.

"No, he's back with Mrs. Cameron, barking at the seagulls." Angus Cameron stuck his hands awkwardly into the pockets of his anorak, and gave her a bright, deliberate smile. "Are you having a good time, then?"

"Great, thanks," said Emily.

"I heard you'd been . . . seeing some sights," Angus said. He looked around at them all with a carefully neutral expression, and a cautious glance at Miss Urquhart. A ring of equally careful blank faces stared back at him.

Jessup said, "Who told you that, Mr. Cameron?"

"Your friend Dr. Pindle," said Angus. He looked about him, to make sure no tourists were in earshot. "Not to put too fine a point on it, he told me you all believed you'd seen the Loch Ness Monster."

Tommy said, "I have to warn you, Miss Urquhart, my father is a reporter."

"Just a stringer," said Angus modestly. "I cover the Highlands for a couple of the nationals." He looked back at Tommy, and this time the look was serious and intent. "Be straight with me, now. Is this true?"

Tommy sighed. He said reluctantly, "Yes."

"It's quite true, Angus," said Mr. Maconochie, coming to the rescue.

Angus turned to him, his eyebrows going up. "And you were really there too, Mr. Mac?"

"And Emily and me," Jessup said.

"We were all in the trailer with the screens when Dr. Pindle's cameras were running in the loch," Tommy said. "And on the screen we saw—we saw Nessie. Swimming. The great big body and the long neck."

"Lord Almighty," said Angus Cameron. He shook his head. "I'd never have believed it. All these years I thought it was a bad joke."

"So did I," Tommy said.

Angus pulled his notebook out of his pocket. "Tell me what you saw. I have it from Dr. Pindle but I want your own words. All of you."

Haltingly they recited their memories to him, each acutely aware of the one crucial element that they were leaving out. Angus Cameron might accept a monster, but it was useless to expect him to believe in boggarts; Tommy, they knew, was the only member of his family to whom their Boggart had ever shown himself.

Angus scribbled eagerly, filling page after page.

"But the creature vanished, and so did Harold Pindle's pictures of it," Mr. Maconochie said. He struck a match to relight his pipe. "So I don't know how good a story this is, Angus."

"Without pictures it's not a story at all," Angus said grimly. He put his notebook back in his pocket. "But the first person to get the first picture will have his fortune made. And I hope it will be me. You have cameras with you, of course?"

"Emily has one," said Jessup.

Emily looked around vaguely at the debris of their lunch. "It's here somewhere," she said.

"Well good grief, get it out!" said Angus Cameron. He looked at them all curiously. "I must say, of all the people I've interviewed who claim to have seen Nessie, you lot are the calmest. Usually they're so excited they can hardly talk straight."

Miss Urquhart said quietly, "I saw Nessie once. Out there in the middle, swimming by, head up in the air."

"You did?" Angus said.

She smiled at him. "But that was forty years ago. I don't think you were writing for the newspapers then."

Angus studied them all again for a moment as if he were trying to work out a puzzle. Then he stood up, reaching to untangle the assorted leather cases dangling from his neck. "Just keep that camera handy, Emily. I'm off back to the survey boats. They'll be halfway up the loch by now."

Jessup jumped to his feet in alarm. "Harold's started his survey? Already?"

"Driving Nessie down toward you!" said Angus cheerfully. "Aye, he's been at it since ten. Good-bye all. Keep your eyes skinned. Nice to meet you, Miss Urquhart."

"Good day to you, Mr. Cameron," said Miss Urquhart, but nobody else paid much attention to Angus Cameron's departure. Tense with concern, they were peering out at the loch, craning their necks to see any sign of the Kalling-Pindle expedition on its ominous, optimistic way south.

"There isn't a thing," Emily said. "Just grey water, empty, as far as you can see. Oh poor Nessie, poor Boggart, what's this going to do to them?"

"Where is the Boggart?" Jessup said anxiously. "We have to warn him! Miss Urquhart—" he swung around, looking for her—"that thing you did, the listening, can we do it in reverse?"

Miss Urquhart was getting carefully to her feet, tucking her jeans back into her boots. "In reverse? You mean call him?"

"I guess. If we all focused on him—Emily and Tommy and me—"

Tommy said with bitter dignity, "Not me. I am not a MacDevon."

"Oh for Pete's sake!" said Jessup. "You're his *friend!* Miss Urquhart—could we?"

Miss Urquhart's green eyes contemplated them from the wise, lined face. She said gently, "I think you have been calling him for some minutes already."

"Look!" Emily said suddenly. "Look at that!"

She was staring up over the loch, and following her gaze, they saw a great bird come gliding down out of the sky in a long sideways slant, the end feathers of its broad wings spread like fingers. Slowly it coasted to and fro before them, golden, beautiful, coming closer and closer.

"My stars," said Mr. Maconochie, awed. "It's a golden eagle! I thought you could only ever see them up in the hills!"

Behind them they heard excited cries from a bus-load of tourists who were just beginning to spread through the castle ruins—*"An eagle! Look at the eagle!"* And then suddenly, in the blink of an eye, the bird was gone, and though every watching person felt that it must simply have dropped past the edge of the castle wall, out of sight, there were a few who knew better.

Emily, Tommy and Jessup looked up and around, turning, searching the empty air for any sign they might recognize.

"Boggart?" Tommy said. "Is that you?"

*   *   *

THE BOGGART HOVERED in a whirling invisible little vortex of air over the surface of the loch, looking up at the three anxious young faces searching for him. Then he turned downward, and called loudly, clearly, sternly, through the cold water to the bottom of the loch, hundreds of feet below. It was not a call that any but one creature would be able to hear.

"Nessie! Wake this minute, and pay attention! There are friends up here concerned about you. And about me."

A long low grumbling sound came drifting up from the bottom of the loch. *"It'll be those who were trying to reach down at me just now,"* Nessie said crossly. *"I want no part of it. A boggart doesnae have friends, except for other boggarts."*

"He has family," the Boggart said.

"You said you were my family," said Nessie, reproachful.

"So I am, but you were the Urquhart boggart and there are still Urquharts in this world too. Even if they cannae

live in your castle any more. And there are still MacDevons for me. And I can hear my people calling me, and yours calling you."

"I'm not listening," Nessie said.

The Boggart lost his patience. Up above the surface of the loch, people looking down from the castle were startled to see a sudden squall churn the water, as if a very small tornado had appeared out of nowhere. But the squall was not weather, it was the ferocious concentrated energy of an angry boggart, leaping in the air and diving down to the bottom of the deep cold lake. Nessie felt it coming, and cowered into the mud.

The Boggart had had enough. He drove into the muddy bottom of Loch Ness like an errant torpedo, and he whirled underneath Nessie's great inert bulk and up again on the other side, screeching like a banshee, stirring up a whirlpool of cloudy sediment. Every fish for hundreds of yards around fled in panic. Nessie moaned.

"You big ungrateful git!" the Boggart yelled. "Three hundred years you've been lying there feeling sorry for yourself, idle, lazy, wasting all your boggartry! You know what's going to happen to you now? Coming up that loch there's a row of boats with eyes that can see you and picture you and make your life miserable for every moment of every day from now on! You'll have no peace, there'll be no sleeping sound in the mud for years any more. You'll be poked and prodded from one end of the loch to the other, with no escape ever!"

Nessie moaned, heartrendingly.

The Boggart went on, unrelenting. *"If you're a true boggart you'll come with me out of here, out to the sea, and there are Urquharts and MacDevons who will help you on the way. But there's to be no more skulking around, no more sleeping. The time has come to change, cuz, and you have to do it right now! Or those friends up there will leave you here alone, and so shall I!"*

A large tear formed in each of Nessie's large brown eyes and drifted away in the muddy water around them. *"I'm sorry, cuz, I'm sorry. Don't leave me. I'll do whatever you tell me. I'll try my best, I promise. What should I do?"*

* * *

"WHAT'S GOING ON down there?" Jessup said. He peered down at the ruffled grey water, which was still churning restlessly as if a small volcano were threatening to erupt far below.

"I think the Boggart's cross," Emily said, staring at the loch, concentrating. "I think he's telling Nessie off."

Mr. Maconochie had the rapt expression of someone listening to music faintly heard, played a long way off. "And Nessie's going to . . . going to . . . I don't know yet. I can see a sort of picture—I think it looks like a seal."

* * *

THE BOGGART SAID, more gently now, *"We'll help you. We will. I know you have this trouble with the shape-shifting,*

I know it's hard. But you cannae stay in the great monster shape, because you have to leave Loch Ness and the deep water. It's shallower, the rest of the way—you have to take another shape, until we get you to the sea. And we'll help you, your family and mine, and me too."

Nessie said tearfully, *"I'll do whatever you say, cuz."*

"A seal," the Boggart said. *"Be a seal, and I'll be another, swimming beside you. That's a creature small enough to swim from the loch to the sea, and big enough not to be eaten by any other creature."*

"But the shape!" Nessie said in panic. *"I cannae keep the shape!"*

"You can do it with help," the Boggart said. *"There'll be three minds making your picture, helping you keep the shape in your own mind. Three minds or four, or maybe even five. That's why you must go seal-shape, not boggart-shape. They can picture a seal, but they can't picture a boggart."* He smiled to himself. *"They saw me once, but there's not one of them could say what they saw."*

Nessie heaved himself clear of the mud, and up into the water, with a flick of his massive tail. He said nervously, *"Will they really help?"*

The Boggart said, *"Come along up, and find out."*

* * *

THE CLOUDS WERE growing thicker over Castle Urquhart, hiding all sign of the sun, turning the sky to a mounded layer of white and grey. The air was chill, and in twos and threes the tourists were leaving the castle's romantically ruined tower for the refuge of the bus that stood waiting for them in the parking lot. But Emily and Jessup, Tommy and Mr. Maconochie and Miss Urquhart still hovered at the edge of the grass-clothed outer wall overlooking the loch, waiting, listening.

Tommy saw a pair of tourists veer away from the rest and come down toward the loch: a tall young man and a tall young woman, both in shorts and Fair Isle sweaters. They were talking animatedly in German, and they were both very blond. Tommy frowned, wondering why they looked familiar, wondering how he could send them in another direction. The girl glanced at him without interest, and then her eyes went to Jessup. She stopped short, and clutched her companion's arm, and they both looked hard at Jessup and instantly swung around and hurried away.

Tommy grinned.

Miss Urquhart was telling Emily about the beginnings of Castle Urquhart. It had been built in the thirteenth century, she said, on the ruins of an Iron Age fort hundreds of years older, and Urquharts—and their boggart—had lived in it for most of the time after that until 1689. But then there was the Jacobite Rebellion, one of many bloody arguments between the English and the Scots about whether a Scotsman should occupy the British throne. "So the English blew the castle up," she said. "And it's been in ruins ever since. With Nessie sad in his loch beside it, missing his people."

"With nobody to play tricks on," Emily said.

"No. Though to tell you the truth I think he lost

his sense of fun long since. Boggarts are gay, flittering creatures—they're not meant to spend so long in one great hulking shape."

Jessup and Mr. Maconochie were sitting together, staring mutely at the water. Suddenly, with no warning, a head broke the surface and rose out of the loch, a head the size of a cow's head, perhaps, at the end of a long neck. The neck rose a foot or two out of the water, the head looked at them out of large brown eyes, and then instantly submerged again, as quickly as it had come.

Jessup and Mr. Maconochie yelled, simultaneously. *"Nessie!"*

But by the time the others had looked up, there was only a faint swirl of water on the surface of the loch.

"Come back," Mr. Maconochie said softly, longingly. "Nessie, come back."

The water lay still. But suddenly a small wind blew around them on the edge of the slope, where they sat on the grass-clad rocks above the water; a small wind tugging at their sleeves and collars; a small wind catching up a paper bag from their picnic lunch, and blowing it around in a little flurry, like a toy. It was their own private small wind, existing for this one patch of place and time, and out of it a husky voice spoke, a voice that they could hear but that drew no attention from anyone else nearby.

"Thoir dhomh aire," it said, soft and insistent. *"Thoir dhomh aire!"*

Everybody looked imploringly at Tommy.

Tommy said, "I hear you, Boggart. What do you want us to do?"

And the voice of the invisible Boggart spoke to them haltingly in Gaelic, for longer than he had ever spoken before, the soft guttural words singing low like the breathing of the small wind, and Tommy listened and translated for them. And what the Boggart said to them was this:

"I shall take him through the water to Castle Keep. I shall swim with him and we shall be in the shape of seals. But he cannot hold his shape on his own, he must have you helping him, you thinking him into that shape. Your thinking must make him a seal, all the way."

"Ni sinn sin," Tommy said. "We'll do it."

Jessup said in a whisper, "Our thinking?"

"Our imaginations," Tommy said. The wind lifted the lock of black curly hair that lay across his forehead. "All the time they will be swimming down there, we have to see Nessie in our minds, have to imagine this little swimming seal, every minute he is on his way."

The wind was still whispering around them.

Emily said nervously, "What happens if we stop, if we think about something else?"

Miss Urquhart was looking out at the water. "He will turn back into his monster shape," she said. "And everyone will know where he is."

The wind whispered, softly, soundlessly.

"When do we start?" said Mr. Maconochie.

"C'uin?" said Tommy to the air.

"*A-nis,*" said the Boggart's soft voice. "*A-nis. A-nis.*" It grew softer still, as if he were moving away.

Tommy gave a short hiccup of nervous laughter. He said, "We start *now!*"

NINE

✳

"LOOK!" Jessup said. "Harold's coming!"

They followed the direction of his pointing finger, and saw a line of boats approaching them from the northern end of Loch Ness. Emily counted: there were twelve of them, moving in parallel, slowly but steadily drawing closer. Watching them, she felt she could almost see the invisible electronic net that stretched below them, sweeping through all the water of the loch. She wondered if Nessie could feel it coming.

There was a splash below them, and they looked down just in time to see the shining back of a seal turning in the water, disappearing under the surface, rising again six feet away. Then the seal's head emerged, whiskered, gleaming, and they saw the big dark eyes looking up at them and knew that it was the Boggart.

And beside him, barely visible under the surface of the loch, they saw with amazement the outline of Nessie's enormous body. It was very faint, there under the dark water, and he must have had his head bent down, for there was no sign of the long neck or any other part of him jutting out. But the body was so huge they could scarcely believe they were looking at it.

"We have to help him change shape!" Tommy said. "We have to think him a seal!"

He stared down at the great shadowy mass under the water, trying to imagine it as small and lithe as their transformed Boggart swimming beside it, and so did they all. Jessup concentrated on the seal he could see, the seal that was the Boggart; Emily thought hard of the doglike head, with its liquid brown eyes and dripping whiskers, that had emerged from the sea to gaze at her days before. And Mr. Maconochie, smiling a little, made strongly in his mind an image of the fat barnacle-encrusted seal he had seen basking on the Seal Rocks near Castle Keep.

Miss Urquhart did not put her mind to making a picture of a seal, but concentrated on trying to put herself into Nessie's mind instead. She thought, as if she were calling aloud: *Come on now, Nessie, you can do anything you try to do. You're the Urquhart boggart—here's the strength of all the Urquharts to back you up. Come on now, Nessie, get out of that Monster shape—*

And buoyed up by all that they were wishing him, Nessie let go of his fear and his uncertainty, and all at once his monstrous shadowy form was gone, and instead a second seal was there, swimming with the first.

"Oh well done, Nessie!" Jessup shouted in delight. This was a mistake; it made Nessie think about what he had done. His fear came rushing back, and just as suddenly as it had appeared, the seal vanished, and the huge underwater shadow-shape was there again instead.

"*I cannae let go!*" Nessie whimpered. "*I cannae do it!*"

"*Of course you can!*" snapped the Boggart, beside him. "*You just did! Change, cuz—everything is change! And you'd better change soon, those boats are getting awful close to us—*"

Jessup said anxiously, "Harold's boats are almost in range! They'll find him!"

"Do it again—we almost had it right!" Emily said. "We stopped concentrating when he changed. That's what went wrong. Think, think—"

They forced their imagining down at Nessie's huge monster-form, a huge dim mass under the grey-green water, and Nessie tried his hardest to change—and as they watched, he went through a sequence of the wrong shapes, born out of his nervousness. For a moment he was a humpback whale, blowing a spout of water; then just as they were ducking under the shower of drops, the spout died away and Nessie was suddenly an enormous eel, sliding through the water so fast that they glimpsed the rippling body only as a blur of speed. Then abruptly the movement ceased, and he was an enormous ugly fish, staring up at them from under the surface, wide-mouthed and goggle-eyed, a monstrous version of the surviving prehistoric coelacanth.

Down on the bank of the loch fifty yards away, clutching his camera, Angus Cameron stared baffled at the water, wondering whether he had actually seen a waterspout shoot up for a second, wondering whether it would come again.

The children gazed down at the flickering image of the fish, desperately willing it to change. "Be a seal, Nessie!" Jessup whispered. "Be a seal!"

The survey boats crept nearer, nearer, down the loch. The research assistant in charge of the leading boat, a red-headed Irishman named Kevin, peered at his sonar screen, seeing for a moment a suspicious-looking mass—and then suddenly the mass was gone.

"Sonar Three," said Kevin swiftly into the microphone that connected him to Harold Pindle in the control boat, further back. "Had a sounding at two o'clock, near the surface." He stood up, looking through his binoculars, and shook his head in disappointment. "Nah. It's just a couple of seals."

Ahead of the boats, two grey seals were playing once more in the water below Castle Urquhart. Nessie dived underneath the Boggart and came up again, blowing happy bubbles, sleek and gleaming. The Boggart dived in turn, rolling over, playing with him, but beginning gradually to lead him down the loch, away from the probing sonar of Harold's fleet of boats.

"Quick!" Tommy said urgently. "We have to follow them in the car! The road runs right along the loch—we can be with him all the way till they're safe in the canal!"

"But don't stop concentrating!" said Miss Urquhart sharply as they scrambled to make for the parking lot.

"Keep the seal shape in your minds—don't talk, don't even think of anything else. If he loses the feel of you helping him, he'll fall back into monster shape in a flash."

In silence they hastened to the Range Rover; in silence Mr. Maconochie unlocked the doors and Tommy, Jessup and Emily tumbled into the back seat. Miss Urquhart slipped into the front passenger seat, eyes half-closed, concentrating now as fiercely as all of them on keeping the picture of the two frolicking, traveling grey seals vivid and alive in her mind. Trying desperately to drive safely while mentally seeing seals, Mr. Maconochie steered them through the groups of wandering tourists, swathed now in parkas and mackintoshes against a beginning soft rain, and out on to the road.

Down on the grassy bank of the loch, Angus Cameron juggled his cameras and his binoculars, peering hopefully out at the rippled grey water, shooting pictures of the line of research boats as they came slowly toward him. He clipped on a zoom lens and took a longshot of Harold's research boat, larger than the rest, chugging along behind the others. Sydney and Adelaide, the Remotely Operated Vehicles, hung ready from davits on her deck like large yellow mosquitoes.

Directly below the spot where Angus stood, two grey seals dived and somersaulted on their way toward the end of the loch. Angus turned his camera in their direction, and then thought better of it. He was not interested today in pictures of seals.

"Come in Sonar Three," said Harold Pindle hopefully into his microphone on the parent research boat.

"Sonar Three, anything else on your sonar now?"

"Just seals," said Kevin's voice faintly from the loudspeaker, in a dispirited crackle. "And a few fish diving out of their way."

* * *

WITH THE POWER OF five imaginations buoying him up, Nessie swam confidently down the lake, reveling in his sleek lithe body and the contentment of being with the Boggart.

"This is wonderful, cuz!"

"Keep it up!" the Boggart said encouragingly. *"You're a great little selkie, you're doing just fine!"*

From the Range Rover, Emily craned her neck out of the back window and caught sight of the two gleaming bodies rising for a moment between choppy waves. The wind was picking up a little, as the fine rain grew heavier, and Mr. Maconochie had his windshield wipers slowly flicking to and fro.

"I see them!" Emily said. "They're right down there!" She strained to see more, but a patch of trees was in the way for a while.

Jessup's eyes were tightly shut, his face wrinkled with effort. "Concentrate, Em! See them in your mind!"

Dutifully Emily closed her eyes. The air inside the Range Rover was silent and tense, prickling with effort, like a circus tent where five thousand people are holding their collective breath, willing an acrobat not to fall off a high wire.

Coming in the opposite direction on the road from

Fort William to Inverness, a small white ice cream van was bowling along, on its way to the Castle Urquhart parking lot. Bobby King, the wiry, crew-cut eighteen-year-old behind the wheel, was looking forward to a good crop of hungry tourist children. The Castle Urquhart gift shop sold ice cream too, but Bobby felt this was ice cream of an inferior brand, and he was confident that he would get a great popular welcome when he parked illegally just outside the castle gate, honked his horn just a little, and switched on the loudspeaker that would send the jingling strains of "Will Ye No Come Back Again?" blaring over the parking lot. Just the thought of it made him reach down instinctively for the switch.

In the moment that his hand was off the wheel, a car ahead of him braked sharply to avoid hitting a sheep that had begun to amble foolishly across the road. Bobby caught his breath—braked, swerved—and on the greasy wet road surface his lightweight van skidded into the oncoming traffic on the other side. With a nasty crunching sound it hit the right front mudguard of Mr. Maconochie's Range Rover.

Panic flooded over everyone inside the Rover. In silent horror Mr. Maconochie wrenched at his steering wheel, while his foot thrust instinctively at the brake, and Miss Urquhart beside him let out a small strangled shriek as the impact threw her forward against the windshield. Emily, Jessup and Tommy were tumbled into a heap in the back seat, and the car lurched sideways and skidded to a stop against a grassy bank.

Mr. Maconochie, knocked breathless by his own steering wheel, struggled to peer around the back of his seat. He saw, to his immense relief, three frightened but undamaged faces blinking at him in the blankness of shock.

"Are you all right?"

"Yes."

"I think so."

"I'm okay."

He put his arm gently around Miss Urquhart, who was gingerly feeling the top of her head. She looked at him with eyes that had momentarily forgotten how to focus.

Doors were opening in the cars that had stopped on either side of the road, and two people were already helping a dazed Bobby King out of the battered ice cream truck. Its side was crumpled where it had hit the much sturdier Range Rover, and the cover of the side from which Bobby made his sales had sprung open, scattering bars and sticks of gaily-wrapped ice cream all over the road. A fine rain was still falling, making everyone damp.

A large bald holidaymaker in shirtsleeves and braces opened the Rover's passenger door and carefully supported Miss Urquhart as she eased herself out. "Here you come, hinny," he said comfortingly. "Don't you fret now, everything's all right."

Emily, Jessup, Tommy and Mr. Maconochie climbed out too, on legs whose knees seemed suddenly a little wobbly. They found Bobby King wavering toward them on the arm of a solicitous bystander, his face pale and concerned. "I'm awfu' sorry, mister," he said to Mr. Maconochie. "It just skidded on me."

"Not your fault," said Mr. Maconochie. "Not your fault."

Bobby King grabbed up a handful of ice cream bars and thrust them at Jessup and Tommy. "Have a Skootchy Bar!" he said wildly.

From the road behind them, shouts and squeals rose suddenly from the cars stopped in line by the accident. Looking back, they saw people tumbling out in excitement and running—not toward the crumpled van but across the road, toward the loch. And then they turned their heads, and looked at the loch.

"Nessie!" Emily said, her voice shrill with horror. "We stopped thinking, we forgot Nessie!"

TEN

✳

NESSIE REARED UP over the lake, enormous, terrifying. He was an astonishing sight. His neck and head towered over the nearest of the approaching research boats, taller than a tall tree, and the top of his great body rose out of the water like the side of an ocean liner. For anyone close enough, there was a strong smell of fish and seaweed, like the low-tide stink of a muddy beach.

On the bank, amongst shrieking, pointing tourists and their children, Angus Cameron ecstatically juggled his cameras, taking picture after picture, zooming in on a sight he had never believed it possible for anyone to see. He had switched to his video camera, filling the frame with a wonderful close-up of the huge head and neck, when Nessie opened his mouth, showing rows of alarmingly pointed long teeth, and uttered a shattering bellow like the grunting roar of an angry hippopotamus. While Angus watched and filmed in breathless delight, the Monster moved threateningly toward the approaching line of research boats, and their pattern changed. The nearest boats broke away, fleeing in panic, tossing on the swells that rolled over the lake from the angry churning of Nessie's massive tail. Only Harold Pindle's bigger research vessel, further away, held its course.

The Boggart, changed back now to his own invisible formless self, flittered agitatedly over the choppy grey water, close to his huge cousin's waving neck. For the moment, there was nothing he could do. Like Nessie he had felt in an instant the overwhelming effect of the car accident, the sudden total loss of the support that had been giving confidence and form to the little swimming grey seal. Like Nessie, he didn't know about the car accident itself. He had only felt Nessie's utter panic, and known the inevitability of the disastrous second in which he switched back again into monster shape, rearing up over the surface of the loch.

He hovered around the dripping hole that was one of Nessie's ears, and hissed at it. *"Dive!"* he whispered. *"Dive, cuz!"*

And Nessie, bewildered and lost as an enormous child, lifted his head with one more anguished, helpless bellow and then bent his neck and dived, with a sweep of his powerful flippers, into the deep cold water of Loch Ness.

The Boggart, reluctantly, dived after him.

Up in his research boat, Harold Pindle was almost speechless with delight, the happiest man in Scotland. He had found his Monster, he had seen it, filmed it, photographed it. He danced a little jig with Jenny; he shouted into the intercom microphone that linked him with the scattered gaggle of smaller boats. "Come back here, you chickens! The eighth wonder of the world and you run away from it! Sonar One, Sonar Two, Sonar Three, get back in line!"

Kevin's voice crackled out of the speaker, its Irish accent strengthened by indignation. "Sonar Three, Sonar Three—it's all very well for you in your great hulking boat! Try being a little feller, tossed about out here and like to be swamped or swallowed!"

Harold snorted unrepentantly. "Stand by, chickens! We're going after him, I'm launching ROV One! Stand by, Sonar Three, stand by, One and Two—the rest of you keep on going!" He strode over to a hatchway and yelled out to the deck. "Chuck! Launch Sydney—now!"

Chuck was standing tense and watchful in the stern, where the gleaming yellow form of Sydney the Remotely Operated Vehicle was rigged and ready, hanging from the arms of a davit over the water. He pressed a lever, and Sydney splashed into the loch and disappeared, while a winch paid out a long flexible wire behind him.

Jenny sat pressing switches and buttons, eagerly. In the bank of screens before her, a green square sprang into life, speckled by blips that were the fleeing fish startled by Sydney's sudden arrival.

"Come on, Sydney!" said Harold, watching the screen greedily. "Fetch! Fetch!"

Up on the road, Mr. Maconochie and Bobby King were scribbling on little scraps of paper, exchanging names and addresses, and whatever other details they felt their insurance companies would demand before agreeing to repair the damage to the two cars. Emily, Jessup, Tommy and Miss Urquhart were paying no attention at all. Escaping the kindly ministrations of helpful passers-by, they slipped away one by one to stand on the grassy roadside bank in sight of the loch, staring out at the water, trying to will Nessie the strength to get out of his monster shape.

But Nessie was far below them, two hundred feet down, on his way to the muddy bottom of the loch. He moved blindly, in instinctive retreat, and the Boggart whirled around him like a small agitated invisible fish, trying without success to attract his attention. Even boggart-speech failed. Nessie was in shock, and for the time being his troubled mind was out of reach.

But at the same time, he was being pursued. Looking up, the Boggart could see the glimmer of Sydney's metallic frame dropping slowly toward them through the dark water. He paused, suspicious, and flittered up through the water to investigate. What was this thing that was following Nessie? How could it see him? In this deep water there was no light at all, and fish and boggarts saw the world around them either by the light of a phosphorescence they generated themselves, or by using senses other than sight. Did Sydney have other senses? What were they?

The Boggart began to glow faintly, from the unusual effort of rational thought—something boggarts are not fond of, under normal circumstances. He turned himself into a treacly liquid, denser than water, and flowed all over Sydney's frame, investigating it. He had seen the ROV above the water, hanging from the davits of the parent research boat, and he knew it to be not a creature but a machine—but this was clearly no ordinary machine. Flowing over its surface the Boggart could sense a very faint hum, the tiny vibrations of the mini-computer that functioned as Sydney's brain. It reminded him of something he had heard before, a long time ago; something that had intrigued him, that had worked a great change in his life. What was it?

Boggarts have the worst memories of all the creatures in the universe. Hovering there, glowing, the Boggart tried to remember.

* * *

UP IN THE CONTROL ROOM of his research vessel, Harold Pindle peered over Jenny's shoulder at the little green screen that showed the findings of Sydney's laser line scan. There against the bright green background was the distinct outline of Nessie's monster body, drawn by the invisible laser beams that darted continually out from Sydney's sturdy frame and bounced back again.

"Look at that!" said Harold reverently. "There's our Nessie! Good old Axel—what a system! Keep it focused, Jenny—don't lose him!"

Jenny leaned forward suddenly to another screen, and made a small surprised gurgling sound. "What's that?" she said.

The screen was white and glowing, with a shifting, indefinable pattern moving through it.

"That's the picture from the video," Harold said, puzzled. "But Sydney's two hundred feet under, it's blacker than the pit down there—how can his video camera be picking up light? Have you turned the strobes on?"

"No."

"Are you sure?"

"It's fading," Jenny said. "Look. It's going away."

* * *

THE BOGGART WAS TIRED of trying to remember; he gave it up. The glow that had made him visible died away, and he poured himself once more all the way around Sydney's complex frame, curious, investigating. He came to the junction point where the long tether wire from the parent ship made its way into Sydney's computer. And because boggarts are made up of a collection of electrical impulses of many varied kinds, he put himself into the wire.

Once he was there, he was instantly everywhere in Sydney's system: seeing, hearing and understanding every impulse that came in through the instrumentation, and blocking out any instructions that came from Harold's switchboard in the parent ship. In effect, the Boggart became Sydney's brain.

* * *

ON THE CONTROL PANEL in the research ship, the screen fed by Sydney's video camera was dark again. Jenny pressed a switch, and wrote down some figures on her clipboard pad.

"Back to normal," she said. "It was just one of those flare aberrations, I guess. Won't affect the regular functions. I'll check out the tube when it comes back in."

Harold grunted. His eyes were fixed on a different screen, the green square fed by Sydney's laser scan, which was almost filled by an image of the top of Nessie's huge body. "Have Sydney back off a bit," he said. "He's too close—I want to see the creature's whole outline. How deep is he?"

"Two hundred and fifty feet," Jenny said. She turned a dial. The image of Nessie's back spread to fill the whole screen.

"Wrong way," Harold said.

"But I'm turning it the right way." Jenny frowned, and twiddled the dial. "Come on, Sydney," she said. "Pay attention."

The image on the screen bounced a little, as if the scanner were giving a little skip. Then it moved sideways, to the edge of Nessie's back and then away from it, and instead a cluster of large fish appeared on the screen. They stayed there, swimming at a slow, stately pace, as the scanner followed them.

"Salmon at two hundred and fifty feet?" said Jenny. "That's amazing!"

"Never mind the salmon," Harold said irritably. "Get the ROV under control. It's not programmed to go off chasing fish."

Jenny began pressing buttons and turning other dials, but nothing happened. The image started to bounce again, moving up and down over the stately swimming fish. Harold moaned, and ran his hands through his thinning grey hair, turning it into an even wilder halo than before. He jumped to his feet, crossed the cabin to the hatchway, and yelled to the deck. "Chuck!"

Several figures were waiting patiently on the deck, swathed in bright orange parkas against the rain. One of them raised an arm.

"Put Adelaide over the side!" Harold shouted. "Right now! And watch her winch like a hawk—we've got a communications problem with Sydney!"

Chuck waved his arm, shouted muffled instructions, and from the second set of davits on the deck the second yellow ROV splashed into the loch. It vanished below the surface, leaving a swirl of grey water, and from a turning winch on the deck the thin, tough fiber-optic cable that was its lifeline went after it, down and down.

* * *

TOURISTS STILL LINED the road along the north side of Loch Ness, peering out from under umbrellas and rain hats at the little flotilla of research boats, watching hungrily for a return of the Monster.

"They say it tipped a boat over!"

"And roared like a lion! I never heard of it roaring before!"

"They say it was huge! Bigger than a dinosaur!"

"What d'you mean, 'bigger than'? It *was* a dinosaur!"

"They say—"

The collision was forgotten; the only remaining sign of it a little heap of melting Skootchy Bars lying in the gutter. Bobby's ice cream van had limped away, and Mr. Maconochie's Rover showed no wounds worse than some scraped paint and a dent in the right front mudguard. With the permission and help of an amiable policeman who had stopped to check the accident, Mr. Maconochie had driven the car temporarily up onto the grassy verge of the road where no cars were normally allowed. There they all sat now, he and Miss Urquhart, Emily and Tommy and Jessup, ignoring all traffic and passers-by, thinking of boggarts. Each one sat in silence, waiting, hoping, calling without words to Nessie.

And down on the mud in the loch below, Nessie stirred, hearing them.

But the Boggart was hearing no one. Frolicking through the deep water inside Sydney's small powerful frame, he was having the time of his life. For the first ten minutes, gradually discovering the maneuverability of the little submersible, he played as he did whenever he took on the shape of a seal: diving, looping, speeding through the water, chasing the fish. Up in the research boat, the Kalling-Pindle team was appalled.

"Sydney's computer's gone crazy!" Jenny said in anguish to Harold, staring at the dials. "He's roaring about at twenty knots! He's turning somersaults! I didn't know ROVs could do things like that!"

This, however, was only the beginning. The Boggart was suddenly a small child let out of school, released from all discipline, letting off steam. For a boggart, he had been living under great pressure since he had come to Loch Ness. After a lifetime of total self-indulgent freedom, with no relationships but those based on mischief and trickery, he had found himself caught in a state of constant concern about someone other than himself—about Nessie. A sense of responsibility was not something he was used to. It was serious; it was exhausting.

But now he was inside Sydney; now he had a toy, and he pushed his feelings of responsibility entirely away. For a little while now, he could be a boggart again, and *play*.

When he was bored with merely zooming and somersaulting through the water, he began to pour himself into the devices through which the sturdy little ROV communicated with the research ship: the video camera fitted behind a heavy glass panel in Sydney's bow, and the laser-scan device strapped to Sydney's back. The camera came first; investigating it, the Boggart sniffed disdainfully when he found it could transmit only the pictures that it saw. *That* was something he could put right at once.

"Harold!" said Jenny nervously, up in the research ship control room. "Sydney's video screen is doing its own thing again!"

Harold was watching the control screens that were receiving images from the other Remotely Operated

Vehicle, Adelaide, as it coasted down through the water in pursuit of the Monster. He glanced reluctantly across at the screen in front of Jenny, and then blinked.

"What's that?" he said.

"I think it's a daffodil," said Jenny.

"A *daffodil?*"

"Now it's a tulip," Jenny said unhappily. "Five tulips, all in a row. Pink ones."

Harold got to his feet and stood looking over her shoulder. In quick succession, the little video screen showed them a clump of white narcissus, a close-up of a red anemone, and a bright blue cluster of grape hyacinths. The Boggart, down in the cold depths of the loch, was feeling nostalgic for spring.

"I don't believe this!" Harold said.

"And it's summer—they aren't even in season," said Jenny. She reached up to her shoulder, and began tugging nervously at the end of her black ponytail. The fingers of her other hand darted to and fro over the buttons of the computer keyboard that sent instructions to Sydney, and the computer paid no attention at all.

"What moron has fed a bulb catalog into Sydney's memory?" said Harold. "Was it you?"

"Of course not!" Jenny said crossly. Fingers flying over the keyboard, she began hunting for flower pictures in the computer, but by now the Boggart had grown bored with spring flowers and was wishing he could be with his favorite butt for tricks, William.

"That's a dog!" said Harold, staring at the screen.

"A golden Lab," Jenny said. She gave a slightly hysterical giggle. "Maybe now it's the Kennel Club listings. Next we'll get a poodle, and a greyhound, and a cocker spaniel."

But all they saw, out of the Boggart's memory, was a front view of William, with his big brown eyes and golden eyelashes, and the long red tongue dangling over the white teeth. He looked as though he were laughing at them. Then William vanished, and the screen was abruptly dark.

Down in the loch, the Boggart, hovering deep inside Sydney the ROV, had seen a light approaching him through the water. He forgot instantly what he was doing, and zoomed up to investigate—and as if he were approaching a mirror he saw Adelaide, the twin ROV, coming down toward him. Two headlamps were beaming out from the front of her yellow frame. Delighted, the Boggart moved to meet her, but Adelaide paid him no attention. Her video camera picked him up briefly, and then passed him by. With her lights reaching out into the darkness, she sailed on through the water on the quest for which she had been programmed: the pursuit of the Monster.

"She's right by Sydney!" said Harold, gazing now at the screen showing him the picture from Adelaide's video camera. "Let's turn her round and see what's wrong with him." He pressed switches and buttons, and the picture swung around to pick up Sydney again.

Jenny and Harold both peered intently at the close-up, as the picture showed every side of the little ROV.

"Looks perfectly normal," Harold said.

"I sure don't see any damage."

"It must just be the—*whoops!*"

Below them, the Boggart, looking out through Sydney's video-eye, watched Adelaide slowly circling, her headlamps illuminating him, her video camera dutifully recording his image and sending it up along her tether-wire to Harold's screen. He chuckled, waiting for her to finish moving around him. Clearly this was some solemn dance performed by ROV vessels while under the water: a kind of ritual communication, suitable for machines. But it was rather dull; it needed a little jazzing up, a touch of boggartry. He watched as Adelaide circled back to the place where she had started. And then he dived at her.

Harold had no time to work out what to do to Adelaide's controls. All he saw was the flashing image of Sydney—controlled of course by the Boggart—crossing and recrossing the screen, and a whirling as Adelaide's camera itself spun crazily about. Not in a hundred years could he have been brought to believe that one of his Remotely Operated Vehicles was dancing with the other, to the tune of an old Scottish reel called "Highland Mary."

Inside Sydney, the Boggart whirled happily round and round Adelaide, singing as he went. He was enjoying himself more than he had for weeks.

But by the time he finally grew bored with his dancing, and the picture on the screen in the research vessel slowed out of its frenzy, something else had happened below the surface of the loch that Harold Pindle would never have predicted. His two roaming ROVs were inextricably tied together, beyond all separating. In the whirling of his dance around Adelaide, the Boggart had bound Sydney's tether tightly to hers in a kind of braid.

Pausing, the Boggart glanced back at the lumpy intertwined line of the two joined cables. He contemplated it, still humming "Highland Mary," and giggled.

Up in the research boat, Chuck came bursting into the control cabin from the deck, dripping raindrops everywhere from his slicker and his wet hair. "What's happening? Both the tethers have quit paying out—have you told the ROVs to stop? Or have they hit the Monster?"

Harold said despondently, "We're not telling these two babies anything any more—just look at that!"

In defiance of any other instructions given them, Sydney's video screen was permanently showing a picture of Adelaide, Adelaide's a picture of Sydney. As they watched, the two pictures began to bounce cheerfully. Like a child turning cartwheels, the Boggart was turning the two ROVs over and over in the water; when he moved Sydney now, Adelaide had to follow along.

Jenny said, "I think their lines have tangled together."

Chuck glared at her. "Impossible!"

"I'm not saying it was your fault."

"I'm in charge of the cables and winches and I tell you it's impossible! Those two lines couldn't get across each other unless there was a diver down there moving them deliberately."

"Stop!" said Harold, standing up abruptly, and narrowly avoiding bumping his head on the roof of the cabin. "Shut up, both of you! This is hopeless—we'll have to bring them back. Try sending a recall, Jen—and Chuck, go start winching them in. Slowly. Gently. *Carefully.*"

Chuck snorted disdainfully at this unnecessary last admonition, and stalked out. While Jenny tried hopelessly to send instructions to the computerized minds of Sydney and Adelaide, muffled commands echoed down from the deck. The two winches sending out lifelines to the ROVs came to a stop, then reversed direction and begin drawing the lines in.

And the Boggart, two hundred feet down in the water of the loch, felt the steady gentle pressure and resented it. He was enjoying his new game of playing submarine; it was fun, and he felt he deserved some fun, and was not ready to give it up. As the lines pulled toward the surface, and Sydney and Adelaide began to move, he pulled them back again.

Sydney and Adelaide came to a halt once more. The Boggart chuckled. Then he let out an underwater war whoop, and like two small square torpedoes, Sydney and Adelaide took off—in the opposite direction from the boat.

Among the groups of tourists looking down at the loch from the side of the road, waiting hopefully with their cameras in case the Monster might surface again, there were cries of surprise and alarm as Harold Pindle's research ship suddenly shot into motion and whizzed erratically across the water, on a collision course toward his patiently hovering line of small boats.

ELEVEN

✳

ANGUS CAMERON HAD BEEN very busy in
the last few hours. By two separate special messengers,
arranged at huge cost which he hoped would be reim-
bursed, he had sent his first pictures of the Monster to
the *Glasgow Herald* and his first videotape to Scottish
Television, with a careful stipulation that he himself was
to keep the world rights of each. Since there had been
no time to process either the film or the tape, he had no
idea whether his pictures were hopelessly blurred or
amazingly clear, but his hopes were high.

And the hopes were justified, for in Glasgow his
editors were already composing a front page headed
MONSTER! with a large magnificent photograph of
Nessie rearing up and showing his teeth, and a byline in
big print: SPECIAL EYEWITNESS REPORT BY ANGUS
CAMERON. And his video film was to be the lead story
of the six o'clock television news, at stations not only in
Scotland but in England, Ireland, France, Germany and
the U.S.A. As a result, crews from other television and

radio stations were already converging on Loch Ness from assorted parts of the globe, by train and car and plane, not to mention three assorted helicopters that were whirring their way southwest from Inverness.

Angus did not yet know any of this. He was sitting in a field overlooking the loch, still draped in cameras and binoculars under his rain gear. His gaze was fixed alternately on two things: the loch, for any possible further appearance of the Monster, or interesting actions by Harold Pindle's little scientific fleet; and a piece of grassy land just beyond his field, bordering the road, where his son Tommy was standing with the Canadian children Emily and Jessup Volnik, the lawyer Mr. Maconochie and old Miss Urquhart from the heather nursery. Angus had a sense of unease about this group. They had no apparent connection with the Monster, except for having been among the first people to see it, but they aroused his reporter's intuition. He felt, for no good reason, that they were up to something.

He waited and watched, and the rain trickled down his collar inside his parka. But nothing happened— until suddenly, down on the loch, Harold Pindle's boat appeared to go mad.

*   *   *

STANDING NOW in the fine rain, to stretch legs cramped from long sitting in the Rover, Emily, Tommy and Jessup looked out over the water, silently calling Nessie. Miss Urquhart and Mr. Maconochie were back in the car, but the children knew that they were doing the same thing; they felt a particular closeness, as if all five of them were a small wonderful choir singing the same sequence of notes in perfect unison.

Nessie, where are you? We're here, we'll keep you going, if you'll just get out of that shape and come where it's safe. . . .

Miss Urquhart opened the car door suddenly, and got out. She called, "He can hear us! Do you feel it? He's moving, he's closer than he was—I think he's on his way—"

But all at once they heard faint shouts from the loch, and saw Harold's research ship shoot crazily out across the water as if it intended to ram one of the smaller boats around it. They gaped, in an amazed silence. Even in a world where they had encountered boggarts and monsters, they felt that what they were watching now must be impossible.

On the boat, Chuck was battling for control of a helm that refused to answer, and in the control cabin below, Harold and Jenny fought for balance, and clutched at loose pieces of equipment as the boat pitched and tossed to and fro.

"What's pulling us?"

"It's those crazy damn ROVs!"

"Maybe it's the Monster!"

And below them, the Boggart, cackling with laughter, was shooting through the water in Sydney's powerful metal frame, with Adelaide held fast beside it so that the two combined ROV tethers made a wonderfully durable towline, pulling Harold's boat. Like a thoughtless rider on a roaring jet-ski he caromed through the line of quivering smaller boats, weaving the boat in and out of them slalom-fashion, terrifying every crew but never brushing a single hull.

The loch grew choppy with the boat's zigzagging wake. In his swaying cabin Harold watched boat after boat flash by, inches from his hatchway, and clutched his head and moaned.

* * *

DEEP IN THE LOCH, where he had been listening to the children's silent calling, where he had almost regained the courage to answer their challenge and change his shape, Nessie lifted his head and sensed what was happening. He could feel the Boggart's joy in mischief, like a once-familiar phrase of music not heard for a very long time. He smiled with pleasure, as faint threads of memory stirred in his boggart mind, and he let his great body drift up closer to the surface of the loch. All his instincts longed to join in whatever it was that was causing his cousin such delight.

But Nessie had changed, since the Boggart first woke him out of his centuries of monster sleep. Now he had a dream, the chance of a life of private gaiety and good company in a quiet place, and his Boggart cousin and his new friends between them had offered him the way to make it come true. Nessie felt, in his creaking sleep-slowed brain, that this dream must not be put at risk, not at any price, not even for a beautiful piece of boggartry. And the calling of the children made him feel that if he were ever to find the truth of his dream, the time to go was now.

He called through the water, in the Old Speech without words, *"Cuz! Cuz, where are you?"*

The Boggart was whipping Harold's boat around in a tight starboard turn, just in time to avoid hitting the bank. *"Over here!"* he called gleefully. *"Come!"*

"No!" Nessie said firmly. He drifted closer. *"No, not now! We have a journey to go, cuz!"*

"Oh later, later!" called the Boggart. *"Come have fun—even big as you are, come over here, come see!"* He laughed in delight as a group of boys scrambled up the bank to escape the splashing of the research boat's wake. The boat roared off again across the loch.

Nessie felt a wave of irritation begin to wash through his happy-go-lucky mind. What about the lectures his cousin the Boggart had given him, the admonitions about snapping out of it, giving up a preoccupation, learning to change? Like a nudging parent, like a stern teacher, he had dragged Nessie out of sleep into a sense of responsibility—and now look at him! Look at him! Nessie's tail began to twitch, and above the loch a few people noticed the swirling of the water and thought it the ominous precursor of a squall. They were right, in a way.

For a last time, Nessie called in boggart speech through the water: *"Cuz! Our friends are waiting! Come with me!"*

"No!" shouted the Boggart. He zoomed gaily past

the bow of the nearest small boat, Sonar Three, spraying Kevin with water, and in the control cabin of the research ship a box fell off a shelf and emptied a dozen tape cassettes on Harold's unhappy head.

Under the surface, Nessie uttered a long growl that grew into a roar, casting fear and dread into every underwater creature that heard it, and with fierce strokes of his flippers and tail he shot after the Boggart, across the loch. When he was close to the whirling course of the two linked ROVs and their invisible controller, he put down his head and lifted his huge back out of the water, and Sydney and Adelaide drove straight into it, and stopped.

The research boat slowed as the tether-towlines relaxed their pull, and lay wallowing in the churned-up water. Harold rolled his eyes at Jenny in relief. "Thank heavens!" he said, pulling a cassette out of the collar of his shirt.

Sydney and Adelaide, stranded, perched on the gleaming grey hump that was Nessie's back. To the watchers from the bank, it was as if they had run into a grey island that had suddenly risen out of the loch. Under the water, Nessie curved his long neck around and took their intertwined tethers firmly in his mouth, to prevent any escape.

The Boggart gave a disappointed whine, like a caged puppy. *"You're spoiling all the fun!"* he said petulantly.

"Cuz!" Nessie said. He let go of the tethers, but the lake and the air all around them were full of the sense of his reproach.

The Boggart paused. There was a small silence. *"I'm sorry,"* he said. *"I'm sorry, cuz."*

"Let's be selkies," Nessie said. He could feel the call from the children's imaginations, up on the bank, so strongly now that he could hardly bear to wait.

"Selkies!" said the Boggart happily, forgetting his game in an instant, and he slipped out of Sydney's yellow metal frame and became a grey seal.

And the island of Nessie's back vanished, and Sydney and Adelaide slid back into the water and hung dangling at the end of their tethers, as the head of a second seal rose through the choppy waves to join the first.

On the deck of the research ship, Chuck and his crew emerged from the various corners where they had been hanging on to rails or spars to keep themselves from being tossed overboard. They restarted the winches, and began hauling Sydney and Adelaide back to the boat.

On the bank of the loch, Mr. Maconochie started the engine of the Range Rover, and the children and Miss Urquhart climbed silently into the car, carefully watching the small moving heads of the two grey seals swimming toward the southern end of the lake. They drove slowly down the road, parallel to the loch and the swimming seals.

And in the field close by, Angus Cameron ran to his van, his cameras banging together around his neck, and climbed in behind the wheel to follow them.

TWELVE

✳

A HELICOPTER THRUMMED over Harold Pindle's research ship, tilting, circling, as the TV cameraman strapped into his seat behind the pilot leaned out of the open door and pointed his lens. But Harold was paying no attention. He was far too busy at the control panel inside the ship's main cabin, talking into his microphone to re-establish contact with the line of little sonar-equipped boats strung across the loch.

"Now listen up, all of you—we've got the ROVs back on board now and we're working on them. What happened was, their programming developed a glitch and they just went off at random, and ended up tangling lines and pulling the boat. As you saw. And they hit the Monster, I guess—how many had it on the sonar?"

"Sonar Two, we saw it," said a crackling voice from the speaker. "A big mass, at two o'clock. Then it disappeared."

"Sonar Four, we had it too."

"Sonar Three," said Kevin's voice. "And we had a

154

live sighting too, like you, Prof. Nessie came up, just his back, and the ROVs hit him and he dived. And he was gone, way off the screen. Must move really fast."

Harold said urgently, "Now did anyone behind you pick him up on screen? Sonar Six?"

"Sonar Six, negative. Not a sign."

"Sonar Eight, negative."

"Sonar Nine, negative."

"Sonar Seven—we had him till he dived. But he didn't come past us. Must have gone back to your end of the loch."

"That's where he is," said Harold with great satisfaction. "Right up this end, and he can't come past you ladies and gentlemen without your screens picking him up. All boats hold your present positions, all boats run sonar continually, and I'll come back on when we've got Sydney and Adelaide straightened out. Thanks, guys. Over and out."

He pressed the microphone switch, leaned back in his chair, and beamed at Jenny, who was ravenously eating an apple after hours of much stress and no food.

"And then," he said happily, "we move up on good old Nessie until he *has* to come past us, and we get even better pictures than we have already."

"Couldn't be much better," Jenny said with her mouth full. "The pix we have already are absolutely fabulous."

Harold smiled contentedly. He said: "But now we have a creature we can spend the rest of our lives studying, so long as we can get funding from enough folks like Axel Kalling. And all publicity is good publicity,

Jen. So we have to make sure Nessie gives us lots of lovely photo ops for those guys out there."

He swung around in his chair and pointed through the open stern hatch, and they both gazed out.

On the rising land beside the loch, the first helicopter could be seen landing in a grassy field. Two other helicopters were throatily buzzing up the loch toward the line of sonar boats. And behind them, in the distance, the water was white with the churning wakes of high-speed launches rushing reporters and cameras and tape recorders toward the scene of the Monster's sighting. In larger quantities than ever before in history, the media were descending on Loch Ness.

* * *

BY THE TIME the two swimming seals, and their anxious road-borne escorts, reached the southern end of the loch, the daylight was dying. The fine rain had stopped falling long since, but the sky had remained heavily clouded, and now greyness was creeping over both land and sky. And fatigue was coming with it.

"They've stopped!" Emily said. Sitting by the left-hand window, she was the car's prime lookout to check on the progress of Nessie and the Boggart.

Mr. Maconochie drew the Range Rover to a halt as soon as he could, and they got out and peered through trees at the increasingly shadowy loch.

"I see them!" Tommy said. "By that rocky bit of beach, down below. " He paused, and looked at Emily uncertainly. "They feel—I mean, doesn't it seem to you—it feels as though they're tired."

Emily nodded. "I think they're stopping for the night."

"And so should we," said Mr. Maconochie.

"But what will Nessie do if we fall asleep?" Jessup said, troubled. "He needs us to keep him in seal shape. He'll suddenly find himself a Monster again, and they'll all be after him." He looked back down Loch Ness, to a distant line of lights that had begun to glimmer in the place where they had left Harold and his boats.

Miss Urquhart said with quiet certainty, "I don't think you need bother yourself about that."

"Really?" Emily said. She looked curiously at the clear green eyes in the old lady's timeworn face, and thought again how young they seemed. Miss Urquhart smiled at her absently, and then became suddenly brisk and matter-of-fact.

"I think they're probably staying the night in the loch for that very reason," she said. "So that if Nessie does have the misfortune to find himself huge again, there's deep water for him to hide in. From here on, the water won't be near as deep—but every hour he spends out of monster-shape gets him closer to being able to shape-shift as a proper boggart should."

"Until he won't need us at all," Tommy said. He grinned at Emily. "Well, and a good thing too. I'm getting awful tired of thinking about seals."

Jessup said, "*I'm* having trouble not thinking about food."

"Come, James," said Miss Urquhart to Mr. Maconochie. "I'll show you the way to a campground in Fort Augustus, just up the road. And you can drive me to the house of a friend of mine who lives there, a lady who's never been surprised at anything peculiar I might do, these past sixty years. I'll stay with her—I'm too old now to be sleeping on the ground."

"You're not the only one," said Mr. Maconochie with a wry grin. But he drove them cheerfully enough to the campground, a half-wooded field beside a stream, occupied only by two quiet tents and a small caravan, and he left Emily, Jessup and Tommy there to pitch camp while he took Miss Urquhart to the home of her friend.

Miss Urquhart gave each of them a hug before she left. "You won't need me after this," she said.

"Oh but we shall!" said Emily in alarm.

"Have confidence, my dears," Miss Urquhart said. "And give it to Nessie. Before you know it, he'll be playing in his new home—and I'll come visit you there. After all, he's still the Urquhart boggart."

She climbed back into the car, a small straight-backed incongruous figure with her white hair, jeans and red Wellington boots, and the children were quiet for a while as the Rover disappeared. Then they set up three tents in the unoccupied quarter of the field, and found that it was possible to see the loch if one climbed to the third branch of a venerable but stunted oak tree.

Darkness fell, and Tommy lit a hurricane lamp. Mr. Maconochie came back looking slightly dazed. "Look at this," he said, opening the back of the Rover to reveal a line of large brown-paper shopping bags. "The friend turned out to live in a stately home, and she had at least three servants, and a famous garden, and a very hospitable nature. It was all I could do to stop her inviting us all to a four-course banquet."

"Why did you stop her?" said Jessup hungrily.

In the light from the lamp, Tommy and Emily were opening the bags. "There's homemade bread," Tommy said, "and butter and cheese, and a ham, boy it smells good, and chutney, and tomatoes and little lettuces, and peaches—"

"And half a chocolate cake," Emily said, burrowing, "and lemonade, and a bottle of red wine called Merlot, and pears and apples—"

"Oh my oh my oh my," Tommy said.

"Oh my ears and whiskers," said Emily. They grinned foolishly at each other.

"Did she put in a corkscrew?" said Mr. Maconochie.

"You bet," said Jessup. "And four glasses."

"Just two inches each for you, with water in it," Mr. Maconochie said. "I'm not wasting a good wine on you heathens. Just enough to make you sleep."

And sleep they did, before long, warm in their sleeping bags against the chill damp Scottish night, without dream or interruption until the birds began to musically shout and the light came.

And all the night, in a room high in her friend's tall stately home, with a clear view out over Loch Ness, Miss Urquhart kept vigil at a window, drinking sometimes from a thermos of tea to help herself stay awake, and making a picture of a small grey seal in her mind.

* * *

ANGUS CAMERON WOKE at dawn, curled in the back of his van in a rest area within sight of the entrance to the campground. He groaned. He was cold, hungry and thirsty, and horribly stiff, and there was such an evil taste in his mouth that he was greatly tempted to drive back instantly to Loch Ness, to find a delicious hot breakfast at one of the hotels where his friends from the press would be staying. He wondered gloomily why his instincts had told him so loudly and clearly to follow Mr. Maconochie and the children.

The News Editor of the *Glasgow Herald* had been loud and clear too, on Angus's car phone the night before.

"Where the hell are you?" he had demanded. "I've got Fergus and Jimmy arriving in some field by helicopter, and they need you."

"I'm chasing a lead," Angus said. "A new development."

"For Pete's sake, Angus—you've just broken the pop story of the century and you don't want to follow it through?"

"I'll be right back," Angus said. "I'll keep in touch."

The News Editor had snorted ominously. "You'd better!" he said.

Angus got out of his van, very slowly and carefully,

and tried to stretch his aching arms and legs and back. He took care not to slam the door, nor make any other loud noise. If Tommy found out his father was following him, he would be furious; he would never forgive him.

An alluring smell of fresh-brewed coffee was wafting over from the campsite. Angus groaned again.

*   *   *

IN THE RESEARCH BOAT on Loch Ness, Harold Pindle's joints were aching too, but at least he had hot coffee, made by the faithful Jenny, to greet him at dawn. He had cat-napped all night, in his control-cabin chair or on a cramped bunk, getting up frequently in case a call might come in from the boats that lay out there with lights blazing at the masthead, or from the cabin roof. In each of the sonar boats someone was awake, watching the screen for signs of Nessie making a move, so Harold felt he should be as awake as possible too.

His clothes were crumpled and there was an itchy grey stubble on his chin, but he was buoyed up by the thought that as soon as the sun was up, the boats and the refurbished ROVs could begin a final sweep up the last part of the loch. Nessie would be waiting there, huge and quiet and amazing, and when inevitably they flushed him out, they would this time get wonderfully comprehensive film and photographs; they might even find where he had his den, or nest, if he had one at all. They might even find. . . .

Harold daydreamed on, as a thin mist lay over the still water in the pale light of dawn, and at the far end of the loch a small double wake rippled back from the heads of two swimming grey seals. And Nessie and the Boggart swam out into the narrow, peaceful River Oich, leaving Loch Ness.

*　*　*

NESSIE PAUSED in his swimming, rolled over, and looked back at the grey horizon that was his loch. There was an ache in his chest and a tightness in his throat, and his eyes were hot. These were not sensations he was accustomed to, and he knew that they were connected with the loch, this silent, beautiful, ancient lake that had been his home for so long. He felt somehow that it knew he was leaving, and he wanted to explain.

"*You are a beautiful place,*" he said to the loch, "*and I have been very happy in you. Thank you. I'm only going because I have to. I shall miss you.*"

The Boggart paddled quietly at a respectful distance, waiting for him, and Nessie knew it and was grateful. He looked lovingly back once more at the grey loch, with its wooded hills rising on either side. "*Thank you,*" he said to it again.

Then he dived into an underwater somersault, and came up splashing the Boggart, and they swam on down the river.

Half that day they swam, following the water through the whole great rift that almost cuts Scotland in half, running southwest from Inverness to Fort William, through Loch Ness, Loch Oich, Loch Lochy and Loch Linnhe, from the North Sea to the Sea of the Hebrides.

They swam down the river into Loch Oich, which was tiny in comparison to Loch Ness, and out again into the next river, broadened for boat traffic into the Caledonian Canal.

All the time, Mr. Maconochie, Emily, Jessup and Tommy kept pace with them on the road, holding their minds on Nessie, keeping the picture of him as a seal. Whenever they lost sight of the water, Mr. Maconochie picked up speed and went on until they next found it again, and then they would park and wait for the two steadily moving doglike heads to appear once more around a bend in the river, or through a lock in cautious company with a boat. It was an uneven journey. Partway through the morning they paused for ham sandwiches and apples from the bounty of Miss Urquhart's nameless friend.

The changes in pace caused great difficulties for Angus, who was trying desperately to keep the Range Rover always in sight without being seen himself. Once, he went shooting past the Rover when it was parked, and was terrified that Tommy might have recognized his van. But Tommy was gazing out at the water, rapt. Angus was too preoccupied to have noticed, yet, that the children were keeping pace with the seals. He thought they were making their erratic stops because they were bird-watching. Geese, perhaps, or cormorants, or even an osprey.

It was when they had reached Loch Lochy that he brought disaster on himself. It was a pretty lake, fringed with trees and mountains like a smaller version of Loch Ness. Angus had been driven by hunger to stop and buy a take-out cheese roll and coffee at a roadside pub, and he was driving faster than usual, chewing his roll as he went, for fear that the Rover had gone far enough ahead to be out of his reach. He came bowling around a corner to find a large ROAD WORKS sign blocking the road and directing him into a rest area beside the lake. The exit from the rest area was blocked by a coach full of Japanese tourists, waiting for its last occupants to board after a picture-taking stop. The only other vehicle there, suddenly visible as Angus came skidding around toward it, was Mr. Maconochie's Range Rover, with Tommy and Jessup, Emily and Mr. Maconochie all standing beside it. The back of the car was open, and they were repacking a pile of camping gear that had tumbled apart: Emily and Mr. Maconochie were picking up fallen cutlery, Tommy and Jessup folding a blanket.

They turned, and Angus found himself facing his son's startled face through the windshield. He smiled, sheepishly.

Tommy was appalled. "Dad!"

Since he could think of nothing else to do, Angus turned off his engine and got out. "Good morning!" he said.

Tommy thrust his half of the blanket into Jessup's arms and confronted his father angrily. "Why aren't you back there at the loch with the rest of them? You've been following us again, haven't you?"

The last Japanese tourist scurried into the bus, and its engine roared like a bull. It drove slowly out of the rest area and away up the road.

"Off to see the Monster!" said Angus genially, watching it go.

"You've been following us! Why can't you leave us alone!"

Angus looked at him expressionlessly. He was a great believer in the art of avoiding confrontation by refusing to answer challenging questions. He pointed over Tommy's shoulder.

"There's cormorants flying over the loch. Must be bad weather coming, if they're in from the sea."

"Dad!" Tommy said furiously. "Will you stop treating me like a wee boy! Will you just go off and do your reporting and leave us be!"

* * *

"*I'VE LOST THEM!*" Nessie said in sudden panic to the Boggart. "*Their minds have gone away! I feel my shape going!*"

"*Hold on, cuz! If you have to change, try to go to boggart shape! Don't go back!*"

"*I'm going—I'm going—*"

"*But you've nearly made it!*" the Boggart said imploringly. "*Another half-hour and it's a full day you'll have been out of monster shape—and that will do it, after that you can—*"

* * *

BUT IT WAS TOO LATE. Out in the water of Loch Lochy, one of the grey seals was no longer there, and instead the huge plesiosaur bulk of the Loch Ness Monster loomed up over them. Water dripped down from his towering neck, and the low-tide smell of mud and seaweed filled the air. The loch was not deep enough for him to dive; he stood there belly-deep, helpless, big as a house. It was Nessie in his familiar shape, but no longer now a shape that he wanted. He looked down at the children from his rooftop height and made a small incongruous whining sound, like a sad puppy.

Angus shouted with surprise and excitement. He lunged into his van for his cameras. "I knew it, I knew you were following something—" Frantically he began taking pictures, clicking in delight at the outline of Nessie's head against the sky.

"Angus," said Mr. Maconochie, "leave the beast be. Has it not had enough bothering?"

Angus switched to his video camera, whirring busily, turning for a long slow shot along the lake to reveal Nessie. He was trying to keep his hands from shaking with excitement. "Are you joking? Here this minute is the scoop of the century, and it's all mine—the Loch Ness Monster leaves Loch Ness—"

"Oh *please,* Mr. Cameron," said Emily in distress. "Please leave him alone! He's not really a monster!" Her hand shot into the pocket of her parka as if pulled by a string, and her fingers hit the little fossil shell and rolled it around distractedly.

Angus paid no attention. He was changing the cassette in his video camera, breathless and intent.

Tommy leaned close to Jessup's ear, and whispered. Jessup's eyes widened, and his mouth twitched into a nervous grin. Keeping hold of one side of the blanket that was still draped over his arms, he held out the other side to Tommy, and Tommy grabbed it, and together they shook the blanket open and whisked it up into the air and down over Angus's head and body.

Taken totally by surprise, Angus let out a muffled shout, staggered, and fell down, dropping his cameras, and the two boys jumped on him and rolled him in the blanket.

"Em, quick, get some rope!" Jessup said urgently, clutching to hold Angus's kicking feet. One of the feet caught him on the knee, and he yelped and rolled sideways. Tommy flung himself across his father's chest, pulling the blanket tight around his arms.

Emily dived into the back of the car, searching for anything that could serve as rope. "Mr. Mac, help!" she said. "Quickly!"

Mr. Maconochie stood frozen, staring at the thrashing heap of bodies.

"Quick!" said Emily. Her voice came out in a desperate squeak. She scrabbled in the car, and pulled out a sleeping bag. Tommy caught sight of it as he struggled to hold Angus still.

"Yes!" he said breathlessly. "Brilliant!" He lunged at Angus's feet again, with Jessup at his side. But Angus was a muscular man, for his size, and very determined, and he began jack-knifing his body in fierce, powerful jerks that shook the boys away and threatened to free him from the blanket. Emily dropped the sleeping bag over him, and knelt on top of it, only to be shaken off like a fallen leaf. "Mr. Mac!" she shrieked.

Mr. Maconochie seemed to wake out of a trance, and suddenly he moved very fast. In an instant he was lying slantwise over Angus's shrouded body, grasping his ankles in two large hands, and the children were realizing for the first time that he was not only very tall and lean but extremely strong.

"Get that bag, Tommy!" said Mr. Maconochie firmly, and he thrust Angus's legs into the sleeping bag as Tommy and Jessup held it open. Then he grabbed Angus's arms, which were starting to flail now as the blanket fell away, and held them still while the boys tugged the bag up to his neck, and tied it securely closed. Angus writhed on the gravel like a helpless, wriggling sausage. His face was red with exertion, and very angry indeed. "You're all insane!" he gasped. The top half of the sleeping bag bulged as he tried to work his hands up to his neck.

Mr. Maconochie took off his belt. "I'm sorry about this, Angus," he said, and he knelt—as gently as possible—on Angus and buckled the belt around the outside of the bag.

With his arms pinned to his sides, Angus stopped struggling. "And you a lawyer!" he said bitterly. "I'll have the law on you indeed, when I'm out of here! Assault and battery, and loss of livelihood! The best story of my life I had here, a minute ago, and you idiots scare it away!"

For the first time since the brief breathless scuffle began, they all looked up at the loch.

The water lay quiet and steel-grey, ruffled by a small wind. The seal and the Monster were gone.

THIRTEEN

✳

THEY STARED at the empty water, and then up in the direction they had been traveling. Though they could see a long way up the loch, there was no sign of anyone or anything.

"Did he turn back to a seal?" Emily said. "Where did they go?"

Two cars crackled their way into the graveled rest area and out again, around the ROAD WORKS sign.

"Help!" shouted Angus loudly in their direction, but the cars had gone.

Tommy crouched beside his father and looked fiercely into his eyes. "Dad," he said, "unless you promise not to do that again I'm going to tie something over your mouth."

"I won't promise any such thing," said Angus crossly.

"All right then," Tommy said. He went over to the car and came back with a dish towel. "Pick up his head, Em," he said, looking grim.

"Aargh," said Angus in disgust. "All right. I

promise. What on earth is the matter with you all? I thought Harold Pindle was your friend, Jessup."

"It's complicated," Jessup said.

Another car came through the rest area. This time it slowed as it passed them, and they saw faces looking curiously at Angus's trussed form. But one of the faces grinned, clearly dismissing it as a joke, and the car went on.

"Come with me, Tommy," said Mr. Maconochie. "I think we'd better head off the traffic, before we get arrested. That sign's a leftover—they obviously finished their Road Works days ago." He loped over to the road and with Tommy at the other end, shifted the ROAD WORKS sign so that it no longer blocked the road but instead blocked the entrance to the rest area. Another car sped along the road, without giving them a glance.

Emily was staring up the loch, vainly hunting some sign of the Boggart and Nessie. "They must have gone on without us," she said. "Let's drive until we catch up."

Tommy came and stood beside her. "Are you sure?" he said.

"No," said Emily. She nibbled at the side of her thumbnail. "I can't feel anything about them at all. It's very worrying."

Angus wriggled irritably inside the sleeping bag. "Mr. Maconochie," he said, "you are a reasonable man and this whole thing is ludicrous. Will you please let me out of here."

Mr. Maconochie was lighting his pipe, sending up a

cloud of blue smoke to be blown sideways by the breeze. He sat down beside Angus on the discarded blanket, with his long legs bent up in front of him. "Well, I'll tell you, Angus Cameron," he said, "it is a very strange sensation for a man of the law to find himself breaking the law, but this is a particular situation, you see. Your son and Emily and Jessup and I are very much concerned that nobody, nobody at all in the world, should know that Nessie has left the loch. We think he deserves a quiet life."

"Why?" said Angus. "Good grief, man, it's amazing that the Monster exists! He's an anthropological treasure, he has to be studied! And he's also a huge great creature who could be dangerous—are you seriously suggesting he just roam about the countryside?"

"No," Mr. Maconochie said. He ran one hand distractedly through his thick grey hair and stood up.

"You're going to have to tell him, Mr. Mac," Tommy said. "He's more likely to believe it if it comes from you."

"You're all daft," said Angus Cameron with conviction. "All the four of you."

Mr. Maconochie took his pipe out of his mouth and blew out a plume of smoke. "The thing is, Angus," he said, "Nessie's not a plesiosaur, or even a monster. He's not a dangerous great huge creature. He's . . . magic."

Even lying trussed on the ground, even with only his head visible, Angus Cameron was able to express absolute and complete scorn in one word. "Magic!" he said.

"He is!" said Emily.

"You've lost your marbles," said Angus.

"A magical invisible creature," said Emily, "with no shape except the shape he chooses. And he changes that any way he wants, like from a monster to a seal."

Jessup said, "He's a boggart. And he's with another boggart, who's been our friend for years."

Angus snorted. "There's no such things as boggarts!" he said.

There was a faint sound over the loch, like the wind blowing in the trees, and the blanket that was lying on the ground beside Angus rose up into the air. Hanging vertically in the air, it moved around Angus in a circle, counter-clockwise.

Angus watched it. His eyes moved suspiciously from Tommy to Emily to Jessup. He said, "How are you doing that?"

The blanket flipped up into the air, folded itself into a neat pile, and put itself into the back of the car. The children and Mr. Maconochie stood very still, watching, beginning to smile. They saw Angus's eyes widen in wonder, and then the look in them changed subtly, and became fear.

At his neck, the sleeping-bag strings tied so firmly and carefully by Tommy were undoing themselves. When they were loose, the belt that was buckled around the bag drew itself out of the buckle and dropped away, and Angus sat up, jerkily, as if he were being pulled. The sleeping bag peeled itself away from his shoulders and arms, and then in an instant he was drawn to his feet, like a marionette pulled by invisible strings. The sleeping bag dropped away, and he stepped out of it. There was no change in expression on his face at all; it was frozen in apprehension.

A car hummed by, on the road, and was gone.

The loch was very still now; the breeze had dropped, and the leaves hung motionless on the trees. Angus was standing on the grass between the rest area and the bank of the loch; they saw him raise his arms wide and hold them outstretched, facing the water, as if unseen hands were grasping his own. They heard a voice murmuring softly, so softly they could not make out what it said, though Tommy said afterward that it was speaking the Gaelic. They saw the fear fade out of Angus's face, and all the tension relax, so that he looked younger, and tranquil, and eager.

And then they saw him fly.

He rose up into the sky, arms still held wide; slowly at first and then more swiftly. His body tilted forward and like a coasting bird he lay in space, rising, rising, banking first to one side and then the other. The children and Mr. Maconochie watched him enviously, trying to imagine how he must feel, what he could see; knowing that the two boggarts, invisible, were up there holding his hands in theirs, carrying him through the air.

Out over the loch Angus flew, and grew smaller and smaller, until they could scarcely see him. He was a smudge against the mounded clouds, a tiny speck in the grand sweeping landscape of purple-brown mountains, dark trees and glinting loch. They watched and watched, holding their breaths, caught in wonder. Then just when they thought they could no longer see him, he grew larger again, coming back, flying.

He flew along the loch, swift and yet motionless. Then he swooped around in a great arc and came back toward them, arms wide still, lying on the air. A seagull flapping lazily over the loch veered toward him, inquisitive, and then dived away in alarm. Angus flew low over the still grey water, rose high over the treetops, banked back again, and then he came toward them over the water, and his legs dropped downward, as the legs of a bird come down to the vertical when it is about to land.

And in the next moment he was stumbling forward, up the small stony beach that edged the loch, onto the grass where they stood. His arms were down at his sides again, and his face was alight with a joy none of them had ever seen on a face before.

"It was my dream!" Angus Cameron said. "When I was a boy, I used to dream I was flying. Up in the sky, like that, lying on the wind, up over the trees and the fields. It was a wonderful dream, I had it three or four times, I never forgot it. But then it went away."

Emily said softly, "The boggarts gave it back to you again."

Angus looked at her vaguely, as if he were not properly seeing her. His face was still caught in wonder.

"You're a lucky man, Angus," said Mr. Maconochie.

"And you don't deserve it," Tommy said.

"I don't," Angus said. He put his hand on Tommy's shoulder. "It's true, I don't. Nessie was talking to me, up there. And the other fellow too."

He came up the grassy slope, walking a little unsteadily, like a man who has not quite got his land-legs back after a long voyage at sea, and he went to where his cameras were lying on the ground, near the crumpled sleeping bag. He picked up the still camera, opened it, and pulled out the exposed strip of film from its reel so that it was instantly spoiled. Then he took the cassette of film out of the video camera and threw it in the loch.

"I took Nessie's picture in Loch Ness," he said. "And so far as the world knows, that's where he'll always be."

"And nobody else will ever take a picture of him again," Jessup said.

"I never thought of that," Angus said. He grinned. "You're right. I'm a lucky man right enough." Then the grin faded, and he looked slowly around at the four of them, Emily, Jessup, Mr. Maconochie and his own son Tommy. "And I ask you all to forgive me," he said, "because you have been seeing the far shore of truth while I have been blind as a bat. It's an amazing thing you've done."

"Put that in writing," Tommy said. "I may need to use it against you some day."

Very close, a car horn hooted, and they all jumped, and looked up hastily at the rest area. But there was no other car in sight: only Mr. Maconochie's Range Rover and Angus's battered van. All the doors of the Rover were open, and for a moment they thought they saw a blur of brightness in the driver's seat. Then it was gone, and the sleeping bag lying on the ground before them rose into the air and moved toward the car. It disappeared into the back, folded over neatly by invisible hands, and the rear door closed. The horn sounded again, an insistent little blip.

"I think we're being invited to go home," Mr. Maconochie said. "With passengers."

Jessup said, "I wonder what finally got Nessie able to find his boggart-shape. And to stay there."

Emily fingered the fossil shell in her pocket, and it moved a little under her fingers, but she said nothing.

"All the great tricks he and the Boggart are planning, probably," Tommy said. "Have you thought what it's going to be like living with two of them?"

Mr. Maconochie grinned. "When the weather's good they'll be out playing with the seals," he said. "And the rest of the time, they're welcome in Castle Keep, tricks and all. After all, they were around long before the MacDevon or me."

FOURTEEN

❋

HAROLD PINDLE stood on his improvised platform outside the trailers of the Kalling-Pindle Research Project, facing a small forest of microphones and a crowd of reporters and cameramen. He still wore his jeans and sweatshirt, but with a clean shirt underneath. Lights flashed, voices shrieked.

"Harold! Look this way!"

"Over here, Professor!"

"Professor Pindle, what are your plans for the next survey?"

"We start tomorrow," Harold said happily. "Just the same as before—we'll go from one end of the loch to the other, with sonar and the ROVs."

"How soon d'you expect to meet the Monster again, Professor?"

"Your guess is as good as mine. He could be anywhere. But one thing we're sure of now—he's down there!"

"Have you definitely identified Nessie as a plesiosaur?"

"It certainly seems likely," Harold said, with his broad open smile. "Until we get close enough to check out his DNA."

"You have plans to do that?"

"You bet. My assistants and I are all qualified divers."

"Professor, the roads round Loch Ness are jammed with sight-seers, and there are a lot of boats out there. A number of people have even started diving. Isn't this going to get in the way of your research?"

"We're appealing to the good sense of the general public to keep clear of our survey," said Harold Pindle, raising his voice a little as a helicopter flew by.

"Dream on, Harold," said one reporter to another, under his breath. "Dream on."

* * *

IN GOTEBORG, Sweden, a reporter from BBC Radio was interviewing Axel Kalling. She had arranged to meet him on the waterfront, for the authentic sound of sea-gulls in the background.

"Mr. Kalling, you must be very gratified by the amazing results of your expedition."

"Most glad, yes," said Axel Kalling, dapper and immaculate in one of his old-fashioned suits. He smoothed back his white hair as it was ruffled by the sea breeze, and smiled at the reporter. "I have always had confidence in Worm."

"It's good of you to make time for us—I know you're

about to get the next ferry on your way to Loch Ness."

Axel Kalling twinkled at her. "No problem," he said. "I am always glad to talk to pretty girl."

The reporter, who was very young and trying to be dignified, frowned a little. She said severely, "You must be greatly looking forward to your first sight of the Monster."

"It is shy Worm, you must understand," said Axel Kalling. "It may not wish to be seen so often, but to stay at home with Mrs. Worm."

The reporter blinked. "Mrs. Worm?"

"And all the little Worms," said Axel Kalling roguishly.

"Uh," said the reporter. "Uh—yes, of course."

* * *

"MR. MASON," said the television talk-show host to Chuck, under the hot lights of the Edinburgh studio, "what do you feel about your sponsor's announcement that the Monster may have a family?"

"You mean Axel?" said Chuck from his seat on the uncomfortable sofa. "Axel Kalling is a great guy, a terrific guy, but not a scientist."

The host looked at Jenny, who sat next to him in an equally uncomfortable armchair. "Miss Wong?"

"It's Professor Pindle's call," said Jenny. " I do have to say it's not exactly likely that a single plesiosaur would have survived in Loch Ness since the Jurassic Age. There have to have been generations."

"So there might be more than one Monster in Loch Ness?"

"Ask us next week," said Jenny with her disarming smile. "But we do know that there is certainly one."

And the screen showed, for the hundredth time that week, Angus Cameron's unbeatable classic picture of Nessie rearing up over the surface of Loch Ness, teeth bared, head and long neck arching out against the sky.

* * *

IN HER COTTAGE next to the nursery, Miss Urquhart got up and turned off the television set, and then the living room lights as well. She crossed the darkened room, opened the French doors, and went out onto her little paved terrace. It was edged with pots of heather and herbs, and when she looked out from it, she could see Loch Ness and the mountains beyond.

On a cloudy night, there was never anything but darkness to be seen, with a prickle of lights from the houses on the opposite side of the loch. But tonight a half-moon hung bright in the sky. In its colorless light she saw the whole distinct picture of sky, dark mountains, the star-scatter of houses on the opposite shore, and the glimmering water of the loch, edged below by the broken-toothed outline of Castle Urquhart's ruined remains.

Miss Urquhart looked down at the castle, and then she turned toward the west. For a long time she looked out beyond the loch, out at the western skyline, where the end of Argyll's great rift lay, and Loch Linnhe, and Castle Keep, and the sea.

"Good night, Nessie," she said. "Be happy. Don't be homesick. We're still here."

* * *

IT WAS BRIGHT MORNING in the Camerons' village shop, and Tommy had gone off early in his little puttering boat to take the morning paper to Castle Keep. His mother stood at the counter of the post-office corner of the shop, her glasses on her nose, checking the weekly accounts. She added up a column of figures, stared at it, blinked, and reached for her calculator.

Angus Cameron came into the shop from upstairs, pulling on his jacket on his way out to the van. He was whistling. He reached across the counter, tilted his wife's face upward and kissed her on the nose.

"I'm going fishing with Johnny Mackay," he said. "I'll bring a couple home for dinner."

"I hope you'll bring a great many home, that we can sell for other people's dinners," said Mrs. Cameron, smiling. She glanced down at her accounts. "Though I must say, we've made more money from your Nessie pictures in the last week than the shop made all year."

"Aye," said Angus noncommittally. He took his fishing rods from a corner behind the counter.

Mrs. Cameron looked at him curiously. "Are you not going back to Loch Ness?" she said. "The whole world's waiting for the next sight of the Monster, and you haven't been there for a week."

"Oh, I've done my Nessie story," said Angus easily. "I'll leave it to the rest of them now. See you later, love."

He ambled out, and Mary Cameron watched him go with an affectionate, resigned smile. That was her

Angus: easygoing, seldom excited, even by the Loch Ness Monster. After all, for twenty-five years they had lived here with a real live boggart just across the water, and though she felt Tommy was very well aware of his existence, she knew Angus had never even noticed. And she was sure he never would.

But then, Mrs. Cameron had not seen Angus fly.

*   *   *

TOMMY, JESSUP AND EMILY were perched over the water's edge at the far end of the Port Appin promontory, with parkas and jackets under them against the wet of the seaweed that mounded the rocks. They were watching the choppy grey-green sea, and the glistening Seal Rocks beyond, for a sight of Nessie and the Boggart.

Six days before, they had arrived back at Port Appin with Mr. Maconochie, and driven straight to the stretch of gravel shore that served as parking lot for the Camerons' shop. It was raining, but there was no wind. As they unloaded the Range Rover beside the little jetty where Mr. Maconochie's dinghy was waiting, they had been aware for an instant of a shimmering in the air beside the car's open door. And then, out in the channel between the jetty and Castle Keep, they had seen the gleaming heads of two seals, swimming away.

Today the rain was gone, and out of a cloud-patched blue sky the sun glinted on the rocks and the small breaking waves.

"There!" Jessup said suddenly.

He pointed, and beside the Seal Rocks they saw a big dark seal swimming. He hauled himself clumsily out of the water onto the rock, and then a second and a third came after him. The third shook his head like a wet dog, and they saw the sunlight glitter on the drops of water spraying from his whiskers.

"It's not them—it's the real seals," Jessup said in disappointment.

"I love the real seals," Emily said reproachfully. Suddenly she shifted a little on the rock, and winced. "Ow!" she said.

Tommy leaned sideways, to look at her. "What's the matter?"

"I'm sitting on a pebble—*ouch!*" Emily scrambled to her feet on the seaweed-covered rock, clutching at Tommy's curly head as she almost lost her balance.

"Something stung me!" she said, rubbing the back of her thigh. Then she realized that her other hand was still buried in Tommy's dark curls, and that he was sitting very still. She took it away hastily. "Sorry," she said.

"Felt nice," said Tommy mildly. He picked up the parka she had been sitting on, handed it up to her, and inspected the seaweed on the rock underneath. "Can't see anything. Maybe a crab nipped you."

Emily took the parka, and found a small hard lump in it, with a sharp edge that seemed almost to send a current up into her hand. She investigated the pocket. "No—it was this! My little shell."

The fossil cockle shell lay in her palm, gleaming white in the sunshine.

Over on the Seal Rocks, the biggest seal splashed into the water. His head reappeared, and to their delight and astonishment he swam toward them, crossing the few yards of water that lay between the rocks and their own promontory. The two other seals rolled off the Seal Rocks after him, but did not follow; they stayed back in the water, watching him.

Nosing along the rocky shore, the big seal found a place where he could haul himself up over the mounds of brown bladder wrack seaweed on to the rock. The children could hear him puffing, like a tubby old man. He was very close to Jessup, who sat motionless, gazing at him, frozen with excitement.

But the seal was looking at Emily.

Emily looked back into the big black eyes, entranced. It was like meeting a longlost friend, it was like talking and talking, though what she and the seal were saying to each other she had no idea. She felt a prickling in the palms of her hands. The big seal lurched a little closer to her.

And suddenly Emily knew what he was telling her. She glanced down at the shell lying in the palm of her hand, and then she looked up wide-eyed at Tommy.

"The seals helped us," she said softly. "They helped Nessie. They gave me the shell, and so it was in my pocket, and three times they made me hold it. I remember now, it was like the shell calling me. Three magics, to make Nessie disappear. And I didn't even know."

"Maybe if you'd known, it wouldn't have worked," Tommy said. "You were needed for a different magic."

"*We* were needed," Emily said.

Tommy smiled a little. He was watching the seal. He said in a whisper, "I think now he wants it back."

The seal was still gazing into Emily's face, calm and patient, waiting for her. Very slowly and carefully, she moved forward on the rock and held out her hand to him, with the shell on her fingertips. She could feel Tommy poised to grab her in case she might slip.

The seal took the shell; she felt his lips cold against her fingers. He looked at her for a moment again, and then he turned and lumbered back toward the edge, sliding into the water with a great splash.

They all flinched instinctively away, shouting with laughter as the water half-drenched them, and it was only as they wiped their eyes, blinking the saltiness away, that they saw the shimmering in the air around them, the blurring of the real world as the Old Magic moved briefly through it. And through the soft regular breathing of the waves against the rock, they heard a thread of a voice, or perhaps it was two voices, faint, musical.

"*Tapadh leibh. Thank . . . you. Tha ar cridheachan maille ruibh.*"

And they saw five seals in the water now, swimming and playing—for two silvery doglike heads had joined the first three. They dived and resurfaced, over and over, the glistening bodies rolling in and out of the waves, and not Emily nor Jessup nor even Tommy Cameron could tell Nessie and the Boggart from the seals.

"It was that same thing he said before, wasn't it?"

Jessup said. "When he showed us himself."

"Aye," Tommy said. "But this time it was double. *Our hearts are with you.*"

"The same to you, our Boggart," said Emily softly. "Same to you, Nessie."

The small waves washed against the rock, echoes of great North Atlantic rollers from out beyond the lochs and the islands, and together the grey seals played in the western sea.

B̲the̲oggart &
B̲the̲oggart and the Monster

BY SUSAN COOPER

ABOUT THE BOOKS

"As long as writers with Susan Cooper's skill continue to publish," the *New York Times* observed, "magic is always available." And magic—the magic of the old ways and the modern wizardry of our new technologies—is at the heart of this distinguished pair of fantasies. In their first adventure, *The Boggart*, Emily Volnik and her brother, Jessup, inadvertently transport an ancient spirit from his ancestral castle in Scotland all the way to their home in Toronto. A mischievous creature, mostly invisible but also able to shape-shift at will, the boggart gleefully runs amok amongst the gadgetry of his new world—until he realizes how much he misses his old one. "A lively story," announced *School Library Journal* in its starred review, "compelling from first page to last, and a good bet for a read aloud." Its equally acclaimed sequel, *The Boggart and the Monster*, finds the boggart back in Scotland, trying to revive the magical powers of his long-lost cousin, the Loch Ness monster. "The play has plenty of sparkling complications," wrote *Booklist*. "The clever premise and great characters will leave kids clamoring for more."

DISCUSSION TOPICS

1. Early on in *The Boggart*, the creature is described as "one of the Old Things of the world not made for human warmth. . . . A boggart, by his nature, feels warmth for no one." Yet this boggart also seems very human, even childlike, at times. What are some of the emotions he experiences? How do his emotional attachments and needs guide his behavior?

2. Why are most of the adults depicted in these novels reluctant to believe that the boggart exists? Would you also be skeptical? Why or why not?

3. The boggart is stung when Emily asks him to avoid getting her and her brother into trouble in *The Boggart*. "Didn't the girl know that boggarts live for mischief, not for harm?" What is the difference between mischief and harm? Does the boggart always understand the difference? Do you or your friends?

4. How could the boggart and the MacDevon clan, which includes modern day members Emily and Jessup Volnick, be related to each other? What is the old legend that links them?

5. Boggarts never die. What are the advantages of immortality? What are the disadvantages?

6. Even though he is an ancient creature, the boggart has a special affinity for computers. Jessup speculates that is because both the computer and the boggart are primarily made up of electrical impulses. What do you think? Could there be other reasons for the boggart's attraction to computers?

7. In his second adventure, the boggart seems more willing to communicate with humans. How does he do it? Why does he do it? Does he trust humans more? Does he need them more?

8. In *The Boggart*, the modern world is described as "a world which had driven out the Old Things and buried the Wild Magic deep under layers of reason and time." Do you believe this is an accurate depiction of modern life? Do you think "Wild Magic" has been buried? Do you think it ever existed?

PROJECTS AND RESEARCH

1. In both novels, the boggart's antics capture the overheated attention of the media. Take note of how the media cover big stories in your community. Do you think the coverage is fair and factual? Do you think some stories get too much attention? Why?

2. On a map, track Emily and Jessup Volnick's journeys back and forth from Toronto to the west coast of Scotland. Be sure to include their stopovers in London and Edinburgh. If possible, map out exact itineraries by air, train, and road.

3. What would happen if the boggart visited your home or school? Would it be fun, disastrous, or a little of both? Write an original story.

4. The boggart sometimes communicates with humans in Gaelic. Find out more about this ancient language. In what countries or regions was it spoken? What language largely replaced Gaelic? Why? Try to find written examples of the language.

5. Imagine that you are a drama critic for a Toronto newspaper. Write a review of the extraordinary performance of Shakespeare's *Cymbeline* that occurs in *The Boggart*.

6. Emily and Jessup Volnik are from Canada, yet they are sometimes mistaken for U.S. citizens when they are in Scotland. The children are quick to point

out their proper nationality. Research some of the social and cultural differences between the United States and Canada. Though the two countries have a long history of friendly relations, are there also points of disagreement? Which country has a stronger link to Scotland and the rest of the United Kingdom? Why?

7. Prepare a feast fit for a boggart. Be sure to include a sampling of all his favorite foods—old treats as well as newfound delights.

TURN THE PAGE FOR A LOOK AT
THE BOGGART FIGHTS BACK

SUSAN COOPER
NEWBERY MEDAL WINNER

THE BOGGART FIGHTS BACK

Out of the cold grey water of Loch Linnhe, the seals hauled themselves up onto the rocks, one by one. There they lay on the wet brown seaweed like large glistening pillows, flippers folded over their round chests, enjoying the sunshine. A herring gull swooped over them and away, watchful, keening its long mournful cry.

Inland, the mountains rose grey-green on the horizon, with cloud-shadows drifting over their slopes. Smoothed by time, the land was like a great hand holding the loch peacefully in its palm—and the seals lay there happily basking in its peace. The small waves lapped at the rocks around them.

And then noise broke in.

Up the loch from beyond the Isle of Lismore a motorboat came roaring, headed toward the rocks, white water foaming from its bow. There were three men in it, hunched down. Banking overhead again, the herring gull saw sunlight glint on the shiny bald head of the biggest of them. Then the shiny head jerked up and there was a shout, and the roaring engine gave a louder roar as the boat and its foamy wake suddenly slowed down.

One by one, the seals slipped into the water and disappeared. The boat swayed there alone.

"Hey—seals!" the big man called out, grinning. "That's a huge attraction, huge! We got a real live Scottish castle and real live Scottish seals! People are gonna just love that!"

"These are called the Seal Rocks, Mr. Trout," said the man at the helm quietly. The engine purred. The boat rocked on the echo of its own wake.

Big bald Mr. Trout stood up, beaming, clutching the windshield for balance, peering at the rocks. "And they're so close by! It'll be a perfect side trip from the hotel, perfect—come swim with the seals, folks! We'll give them snorkels and flippers! Guess they'll need full wet suits too, in this place." He gave a loud snicker.

The helmsman did not smile, but the third man in the boat, younger, laughed heartily. "Great idea!" he said. "Great!" Like Trout, he was wearing a black rain jacket with a large letter *T* printed in yellow on its back.

The helmsman said politely, "Seals are a protected species in Scotland, Mr. Trout."

Trout snorted, and waved his free hand. "So what? Nobody's going to shoot them, man! The seals'll love it too, believe me, I know about these things! Dolphins swim with people all the time at my Florida resort—everyone knows they enjoy it!"

"Absolutely true!" said the younger man firmly, and Trout smiled at him in approval. Then he turned away from the seals, facing the loch.

"And here's our biggest selling point—the castle!" He flung out his arm in a proud sweep toward the very small island beyond the Seal Rocks. It was not much more than a rock itself, but from its grassy back rose the neat square shape of the oldest and smallest castle in all of Scotland, Castle Keep. The water of the loch lapped peacefully around its edge, and beyond it the mountains rolled green and timeless into the distance.

"Perfect!" said the young man. He reached into an inside pocket for his cell phone and began taking pictures.

The helmsman waited in the rocking boat, silent. The engine thrummed.

"We're renting, but it'll be mine soon—just got to clear up a few legal details," Trout said. "Then I might make it look more the way people expect a castle to look—you know, battlements, all that stuff. On the shore, we got two hundred acres now, and there's nothing in the way—just a tacky little store. We're buying that, of course. Perfect! Plenty of room for the hotel and the condos, and all of it only ten minutes from the golf course! I'd buy that too, make it much, much better, a real Trout course—but it's municipal, belongs to the town."

The herring gull drifted high overhead, keening.

"But you got the castle, that's what matters!" the young man said. "I love it! You really hit the jackpot this time!"

"So I want you to get the website up just before we make the announcement, okay? No point in stirring up the screaming tree-huggers before we have to. And they'll be waiting, oh yes—all these fabulous developments I've done, but the lying agitators always try to make me the bad guy." Trout scowled for a moment, then brightened again. "Well, not this time! We'll set up the website with all these beautiful pictures you're taking and then we'll announce—and I want a press conference that very day. Bring 'em all in by bus, buses from all over. Right?"

"Right!" said the young man fervently.

Mr. Trout swung round toward the man at the helm, flashing snowy white teeth in a broad suntanned face. "Okay, Dougal! Show him where the Trout Castle Resort's going to be! Let's go!"

He whacked him happily on the shoulder, ignoring the fact that the shoulder led to the hand on the boat's controls, and again the engine gave a sudden earsplitting roar. Hastily the helmsman calmed it, as the other two laughed, and the motorboat creamed away from the Seal Rocks, round the quiet unsuspecting island where Castle Keep stood.

And deep at the bottom of the loch, far below, a little twirling cloud of sand puffed up into the dark water, as something stirred. Something formless and ancient, which had been sleeping peacefully there in the sandy mud for years. One of the Old Things, a creature bound by no rules but those of the Wild Magic; a creature who might well have slept on for the rest of this century, if that sudden snarl of that boat's engine had not jolted it conscious again.

The Boggart was waking up, just in time.

Tom Cameron closed the trunk of his rented car, and looked out at the little wooden jetty on the shore of the loch. Then he looked past it, across the years and the memories, at grey Castle Keep rising from its green hummock in the great stretch of tranquil water beyond. The jetty hadn't been there when he was a boy, but his father's battered little dinghy, tied up to it now, looked just as tough and indomitable as it had thirty years before.

"That was my boat when I was your age," he said.

Jay said, "You had your *own boat*?"

"With a puny wee motor, though," Granda said. "Mine's better."

Jay stared at his father enviously. "You had your own boat *and* a motor."

Tom laughed, and settled himself in the car. "Don't get the idea that parents were softer then," he said. "Dad was a tough cookie. Until I was ten I didn't have a motor at all—he made me row."

Allie came running from the store with a bottle of Scottish Spring Water in her hand, and reached it in to him through the car window.

"Stay hydrated, Dad!" she said.

Tom Cameron grinned at her. "Thank you, doctor."

"And text us when you get to Edinburgh."

"He can't. I told you, we don't have reception here," Jay said, rolling his eyes. He was the practical twin.

Allie paused, deflated. "Shoot. I'd forgotten."

Their father started the engine. "I'll call you—on Granda's beautiful efficient old landline. And you use it too—call your mom. Often. You know how mad she was that she couldn't come."

"Working mothers!" said Jay, with an eye on his sister. "Huh!"

Allie took the bait instantly, satisfyingly. "It wasn't her fault!" she said indignantly. "She was just unlucky her meeting was in Ottawa and not here!" Then she saw her brother's grinning face, and she punched him.

"And you were lucky that I was luckier," Tom said. He winked at Granda, and started the engine. "Be good. I'll call you tonight. Bye, all!"

They waved as he drove off, along the track that would join the road snaking round Loch Linnhe toward the mountains.

Allie took her grandfather's hand. "Okay, Granda—now you're stuck with us, for two whole weeks," she said with satisfaction.

"Free labor," Angus Cameron said. "And ye'll likely be my defense against the dreaded visitors. The accents will confuse the heck out of them."

To the twins' eyes he was an older model of their father, Tom, this year more than ever: the same lean frame and watchful blue eyes, the same retreating curly hair—though on Granda, the curls were snowy white. For the past five years, since Grammie died, he had been visiting them each year in Toronto; this summer, to their delight, they were here instead.

Granda dropped Allie's hand and gave her ponytail a tug. "Back to work," he said, and he turned back toward the Port Appin Store, with its crowded windows full of everything from whisky to paper clips. Strictly speaking, Granda was a journalist; he had been briefly very famous, long before they were born, for taking the only unquestionably clear photograph of the Loch Ness Monster, still reproduced all over the world. But these days it was the store that earned him his living.

Out on the loch there was a brief roar from an engine, though it rapidly faded. They all looked but could see only the waves lapping at the shore, and the brooding shape of Castle Keep on its little island.

Granda sighed. "Speaking of visitors," he said.

Jay said hopefully, "Can we take your boat out?"

"Later. You can go with Portia. It's Monday—housekeeping day for the castle, until the season begins."

"Yay!" Allie said. "We get to go inside!"

"You get to vacuum, if she lets you," her grandfather said. "Come on, now."

They had met Portia; she was a masterful lady who arrived nearly every day to help Granda run the store and look after the castle, whose distant owners were seldom there. Until its summer tourist season began, the two of them were the keepers of the castle, protective and respectful.

Gulls swooped over the twins' heads as they walked back from the road, across the stretch of grass and stones that would be crowded wheel to wheel, soon, with the cars of holidaymakers arriving to admire Castle Keep. The most patient of these admirers would wait for hours to tour the inside of the castle, ferried over in small groups by one of the local schoolteachers who acted as guides, but many others came just to gaze and exclaim, and to buy snacks and souvenirs at Granda's store, as well as framed, signed copies of his famous photograph of the Monster. He was grateful, but always relieved when the summer ended and the stream of visitors became a trickle.

At the store door Jay paused, and turned for one more wistful look at the loch, trying to remember misty, haunting images from their only other visit to Scotland, when he and Allie had been five years old.

"The seals," he said. "Are the seals still there?"

Down on the bottom of the loch the Boggart paused, in his yawning way back into sleep. He looked up. Very, very dimly, against the faint glow that was all that this dark water would show him of the sunlight above its surface, he saw the flicker of a diving seal. For a moment he remembered the delight of diving like that, taking on that same shape, playing with the wild things.

And there was something else holding him back from sleep as well, something other than the seals; something else was calling to him. It was very faint, but he could sense it. Though there was nothing to see or hear, the call was reaching out to his ancient, magical, formless mind.

What was it?

Who was it?

* * *

In the store, Mozart's first Horn Concerto was playing softly out of the radio, over the groceries, and Portia was standing there motionless, looking worried. She was a brisk, compact person with short grey hair, and Granda had never seen her either motionless or worried before. He looked at her warily. She stood in the open doorway between the store and the kitchen of the house, still wearing her raincoat.

Allie beamed at her. "Morning, Portia!"

Portia was looking at Granda: an odd, strained look. "I'm making some tea," she said.

"That's nice," said Granda mildly.

"Dad took off to Edinburgh, for work," Jay said. "For two weeks!"

Portia paid him no attention. She held up a long white envelope. "I met the postman," she said.

"Portia," said Granda, "are ye all right?"

"There was a phone call for you too," Portia said. "Just now. I didn't realize you were out by the loch."

"Well, that's no problem," Granda said. "I'll ring them back."

"It was a man. He said it was about your selling the store."

There was a sudden silence. Even the music seemed to pause. The twins stared at her, and then at their grandfather.

"He sounded American." Portia's voice shook a little. "Angus, you aren't selling the store, are you?"

"Are ye joking?" said Granda. "Of course not."

She was still holding up the envelope. "And there's this. The man said there would be a letter."

"This is ridiculous," Granda said. He took the envelope, glanced at it briefly, and tore it in half.

"There have been several letters and several phone calls," he said. "And endless e-mails. From the Trout Corporation, whoever they are. I said no the first time, but they keep on and on. Someday they'll grasp the fact that when a Scot says no, he means it."

"They want to buy the store?" Jay said.

"They want to buy this whole piece of coast and nae doubt the castle, and build a resort for American tourists. Can you believe it? Right here. But to my knowledge the castle's not for sale and nor am I, so they've another think coming." Granda dropped the pieces of envelope into a wastepaper basket. "Portia, where's that tea?"

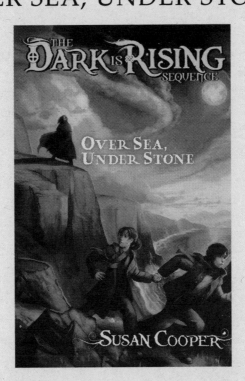

WHERE IS HE?"

Barney hopped from one foot to the other as he clambered down from the train, peering in vain through the white-faced crowds flooding eagerly to the St. Austell ticket barrier. "Oh, I can't see him. Is he there?"

"Of course he's there," Simon said, struggling to clutch the long canvas bundle of his father's fishing rods. "He said he'd meet us. With a car."

Behind them, the big diesel locomotive hooted like a giant owl, and the train began to move out.

"Stay where you are a minute," Father said, from a barricade of suitcases. "Merry won't vanish. Let people get clear."

Jane sniffed ecstatically. "I can smell the sea!"

"We're miles from the sea," Simon said loftily.

"I don't care. I can smell it."

"Trewissick's five miles from St. Austell, Great-Uncle Merry said."

"Oh, where *is* he?" Barney still jigged impatiently on the dusty grey platform, glaring at the disappearing backs that masked his view. Then suddenly he stood still, gazing downwards. "Hey—look."

They looked. He was staring at a large black suitcase among the forest of shuffling legs.

"What's so marvellous about that?" Jane said.

Then they saw that the suitcase had two brown pricked ears and a long waving brown tail. Its owner picked it up and moved away, and the dog which had been behind it was left standing there alone, looking up and down the platform. He was a long, rangy, lean dog, and where the sunlight shafted down on his coat it gleamed dark red.

Barney whistled, and held out his hand.

"Darling, no," said his mother plaintively, clutching at the bunch of paint-brushes that sprouted from her pocket like a tuft of celery.

But even before Barney whistled, the dog had begun trotting in their direction, swift and determined, as if he were recognizing old friends. He loped round them in a circle, raising his long red muzzle to each in turn, then stopped beside Jane, and licked her hand.

"Isn't he gorgeous?" Jane crouched beside him, and ruffled the long silky fur of his neck.

"Darling, be careful," Mother said. "He'll get left behind. He must belong to someone over there."

"I wish he belonged to us."

"So does he," Barney said. "Look."

He scratched the red head, and the dog gave a throaty half-bark of pleasure.

"*No,*" Father said.

The crowds were thinning now, and through the barrier

they could see clear blue sky out over the station yard.

"His name's on his collar," Jane said, still down beside the dog's neck. She fumbled with the silver tab on the heavy strap. "It says Rufus. And something else . . . Trewissick. Hey, he comes from the village!"

But as she looked up, suddenly the others were not there. She jumped to her feet and ran after them into the sunshine, seeing in an instant what they had seen: the towering familiar figure of Great-Uncle Merry, out in the yard, waiting for them.

They clustered round him, chattering like squirrels round the base of a tree. "Ah, there you are," he said casually, looking down at them from beneath his bristling white eyebrows with a slight smile.

"Cornwall's wonderful," Barney said, bubbling.

"You haven't seen it yet," said Great-Uncle Merry. "How are you, Ellen, my dear?" He bent and aimed a brief peck at Mother's cheek. He treated her always as though he had forgotten that she had grown up. Although he was not her real uncle, but only a friend of her father, he had been close to the family for so many years that it never occurred to them to wonder where he had come from in the first place.

Nobody knew very much about Great-Uncle Merry, and nobody ever quite dared to ask. He did not look in the least like his name. He was tall, and straight, with a lot of very thick, wild, white hair. In his grim brown face the nose curved fiercely, like a bent bow, and the eyes were deep-set and dark.

How old he was, nobody knew. "Old as the hills," Father said, and they felt, deep down, that this was probably right. There was something about Great-Uncle Merry that was like the hills, or the sea, or the sky; something ancient, but without age or end.

Always, wherever he was, unusual things seemed to happen. He would often disappear for a long time, and then suddenly come through the Drews' front door as if he had never been away, announcing that he had found a lost valley in South America, a Roman fortress in France, or a burned Viking ship buried on the English coast. The newspapers would publish enthusiastic stories of what he had done. But by the time the reporters came knocking at the door, Great-Uncle Merry would be gone, back to the dusty peace of the university where he taught. They would wake up one morning, go to call him for breakfast, and find that he was not there. And then they would hear no more of him until the next time, perhaps months later, that he appeared at the door. It hardly seemed possible that this summer, in the house he had rented for them in Trewissick, they would be with him in one place for four whole weeks.

The sunlight glinting on his white hair, Great-Uncle Merry scooped up their two biggest suitcases, one under each arm, and strode across the yard to a car.

"What d'you think of that?" he demanded proudly.

Following, they looked. It was a vast, battered estate car, with rusting mudguards and peeling paint, and mud caked on the hubs of the wheels. A wisp of steam curled up from the radiator.

"Smashing!" said Simon.

"Hmmmmmm," Mother said.

"Well, Merry," Father said cheerfully, "I hope you're well insured."

Great-Uncle Merry snorted. "Nonsense. Splendid vehicle. I hired her from a farmer. She'll hold us all, anyway. In you get."

Jane glanced regretfully back at the station entrance as she clambered in after the rest. The red-haired dog was standing on the pavement watching them, long pink tongue dangling over white teeth.

Great-Uncle Merry called: "Come on, Rufus."

"Oh!" Barney said in delight, as a flurry of long legs and wet muzzle shot through the door and knocked him sideways. "Does he belong to you?"

"Heaven forbid," Great-Uncle Merry said. "But I suppose he'll belong to you three for the next month. The captain couldn't take him abroad, so Rufus goes with the Grey House." He folded himself into the driving seat.

"The Grey House?" Simon said. "Is that what it's called? Why?"

"Wait and see."

The engine gave a hiccup and a roar, and then they were away. Through the streets and out of the town they thundered in the lurching car, until hedges took the place of houses; thick, wild hedges growing high and green as the road wound uphill, and behind them the grass sweeping up to the sky. And against the sky they saw nothing but lonely trees, stunted and bowed by the wind that blew from the sea, and yellow-grey outcrops of rock.

"There you are," Great-Uncle Merry shouted, over the noise. He turned his head and waved one arm away from the steering-wheel, so that Father moaned softly and hid his eyes. "Now you're in Cornwall. The real Cornwall. Logres is before you."

The clatter was too loud for anyone to call back.

"What's he mean, Logres?" demanded Jane.

Simon shook his head, and the dog licked his ear.

"He means the land of the West," Barney said unexpectedly, pushing back the forelock of fair hair that always tumbled over his eyes. "It's the old name for Cornwall. King Arthur's name."

Simon groaned. "I might have known."

Ever since he had learned to read, Barney's greatest heroes had been King Arthur and his knights. In his dreams he fought imaginary battles as a member of the Round Table, rescuing fair ladies and slaying false knights. He had been longing to come to the West Country; it gave him a strange feeling that he would in some way be coming home. He said, resentfully: "You wait. Great-Uncle Merry knows."

And then, after what seemed a long time, the hills gave way to the long blue line of the sea, and the village was before them.

Trewissick seemed to be sleeping beneath its grey, slate-tiled roofs, along the narrow winding streets down the hill. Silent behind their lace-curtained windows, the little square houses let the roar of the car bounce back from their white-washed walls. Then Great-Uncle Merry swung the wheel round, and suddenly they were driving along the edge of the harbour, past water rippling and flashing golden in the afternoon sun. Sailing-dinghies bobbed at their moorings along the quay, and a whole row of the Cornish fishing boats that they had seen only in pictures painted by their mother years before: stocky workmanlike boats, each with a stubby mast and a small square engine-house in the stern.

Nets hung dark over the harbour walls, and a few fishermen, hefty, brown-faced men in long boots that reached their thighs, glanced up idly as the car passed. Two or three grinned at Great-Uncle Merry, and waved.

"Do they know you?" Simon said curiously.

But Great-Uncle Merry, who could become very deaf when he chose not to answer a question, only roared on along the road that curved up the hill, high over the other side of the harbour, and suddenly stopped. "Here we are," he said.

In the abrupt silence, their ears still numb from the thundering engine, they all turned from the sea to look at the other side of the road.

They saw a terrace of houses sloping sideways up the steep hill; and in the middle of them, rising up like a tower, one tall narrow house with three rows of windows and a gabled roof. A sombre house, painted dark-grey, with the door and windowframes shining white. The roof was slate-tiled, a high blue-grey arch facing out across the harbour to the sea.

"The Grey House," Great-Uncle Merry said.

They could smell a strangeness in the breeze that blew faintly on their faces down the hill; a beckoning smell of salt and seaweed and excitement.

As they unloaded suitcases from the car, with Rufus darting in excited frenzy through everyone's legs, Simon suddenly clutched Jane by the arm. "Gosh—*look*!"

He was looking out to sea, beyond the harbour mouth. Along his pointed finger, Jane saw the tall graceful triangle of a yacht under full sail, moving lazily in towards Trewissick.

"Pretty," she said, with only mild enthusiasm. She did not share Simon's passion for boats.

"She's a beauty. I wonder whose she is?" Simon stood

watching, entranced. The yacht crept nearer, her sails beginning to flap; and then the tall white mainsail crumpled and dropped. They heard the rattle of rigging, very faint across the water, and the throaty cough of an engine.

"Mother says we can go down and look at the harbour before supper," Barney said, behind them. "Coming?"

"Course. Will Great-Uncle Merry come?"

"He's going to put the car away."

They set off down the road leading to the quay, beside a low grey wall with tufts of grass and pink valerian growing between its stones. In a few paces Jane found she had forgotten her handkerchief, and she ran back to retrieve it from the car. Scrabbling on the floor by the back seat, she glanced up and stared for a moment through the windscreen, surprised.

Great-Uncle Merry, coming back towards the car from the Grey House, had suddenly stopped in his tracks in the middle of the road. He was gazing down at the sea; and she realised that he had caught sight of the yacht. What startled her was the expression on his face. Standing there like a craggy towering statue, he was frowning, fierce and intense, almost as if he were looking and listening with senses other than his eyes and ears. He could never look frightened, she thought, but this was the nearest thing to it that she had ever seen. Cautious, startled, alarmed . . . what was the matter with him? Was there something strange about the yacht?

Then he turned and went quickly back into the house, and Jane emerged thoughtfully from the car to follow the boys down the hill.

* * *

The harbour was almost deserted. The sun was hot on their faces, and they felt the warmth of the stone quayside strike at their feet through their sandal soles. In the center, in front of tall wooden warehouse doors, the quay jutted out square into the water, and a great heap of empty boxes towered above their heads. Three sea-gulls walked tolerantly to the edge, out of their way. Before them, a small forest of spars and ropes swayed; the tide was only half high, and the decks of the moored boats were down below the quayside, out of sight.

"Hey," Simon said, pointing through the harbour entrance. "That yacht's come in, look. Isn't she marvellous?"

The slim white boat sat at anchor beyond the harbour wall, protected from the open sea by the headland on which the Grey House stood.

Jane said: "Do you think there is anything odd about her?"

"Odd? Why should there be?"

"Oh—I don't know."

"Perhaps she belongs to the harbour-master," Barney said.

"Places this size don't have harbour-masters, you little fathead, only ports like Father went to in the navy."

"Oh yes they do, cleversticks, there's a little black door on the corner over there, marked Harbour-Master's Office." Barney hopped triumphantly up and down, and frightened a sea-gull away. It ran a few steps and then flew off, flapping low over the water and bleating into the distance.

"Oh well," Simon said amiably, shoving his hands in his pockets and standing with his legs apart, rocking on his heels, in his captain-on-the-bridge stance. "One up. Still, that boat must belong to someone pretty rich. You could cross the Channel in her, or even the Atlantic."

"Ugh," said Jane. She swam as well as anybody, but she was the only member of the Drew family who disliked the open sea. "Fancy crossing the Atlantic in a thing that size."

Simon grinned wickedly. "Smashing. Great big waves picking you up and bringing you down swoosh, everything falling about, pots and pans upsetting in the galley, and the deck going up and down, up and down—"

"You'll make her sick," Barney said calmly.

"Rubbish. On dry land, out here in the sun?"

"Yes, you will, she looks a bit green already. Look."

"I don't."

"Oh yes you do. I can't think why you weren't ill in the train like you usually are. Just think of those waves in the Atlantic, and the mast swaying about, and nobody with an appetite for their breakfast except me. . . ."

"Oh shut up, I'm not going to listen"—and poor Jane turned and ran round the side of the mountain of fishy-smelling boxes, which had probably been having more effect on her imagination than the thought of the sea.

"Girls!" said Simon cheerfully.

There was suddenly an ear-splitting crash from the other side of the boxes, a scream, and a noise of metal jingling on concrete. Simon and Barney gazed horrified at one another for a moment, and rushed round to the other side.